GEORGE ELIOT

BROTHER JACOB

WITH A NEW AFTERWORD BY
BERYL GRAY

Virago

Published by VIRAGO PRESS Limited 1989
20–23 Mandela Street, Camden Town, London NW1 0HQ.

First published in Great Britain with *Silas Marner* and *The Lifted Veil* by Wm. Blackwood & Sons in a Cabinet edition 1878
First published as a single volume by Virago Press 1989

Eliot, George, *1819–1880*
    Brother Jacob.
    Rn: Mary Ann Evans
    I. Title
    823'.8 [F]

    ISBN 1–85381–040–1

Printed in Great Britain
by Cox and Wyman Ltd, Reading, Berks.

'Trompeurs, c'est pour vous que j'écris,
Attendez vous à la pareille.'
        – LA FONTAINE

CHAPTER 1

Among the many fatalities attending the bloom of young desire, that of blindly taking to the confectionery line has not, perhaps, been sufficiently considered. How is the son of a British yeoman, who has been fed principally on salt pork and yeast dumplings, to know that there is satiety for the human stomach even in a paradise of glass jars full of sugared almonds and pink lozenges, and that the tedium of life can reach a pitch where plum-buns at discretion cease to offer the slightest enticement? Or how, at the tender age when a confectioner seems to him a very prince whom all the world must envy, – who breakfasts on macaroons, dines on marengs, sups on twelfth-cake, and fills up the intermediate hours with sugar-candy or peppermint, – how is he to foresee the day of sad wisdom, when he will discern that the confectioner's calling is not socially influential, or favourable to a soaring ambition? I have known a man who turned out to have a metaphysical genius, incautiously, in the period of youthful buoyancy, commence his career as a dancing-master; and you may imagine the use that was made of this initial mistake by opponents who felt themselves bound to warn the public against his doctrine of the Inconceivable. He could not give up his dancing-lessons, because he made his bread by them, and metaphysics would not have found him in so much as salt to his bread.

It was really the same with Mr David Faux and the confectionery business. His uncle, the butler at the great house close by Brigford, had made a pet of him in his early boyhood, and it was on a visit to this uncle that the confectioners' shops in that brilliant town had, on a single day, fired his tender imagination. He carried home the pleasing illusion that a confectioner must be at once the happiest and the foremost of men, since the things he made were not only the most beautiful to behold, but the very best eating, and such as the Lord Mayor must always order largely for his private recreation; so that when his father declared he must be put to a trade, David chose his line without a moment's hesitation; and, with a rashness inspired by a sweet tooth, wedded himself irrevocably to confectionery. Soon, however, the tooth lost its relish and fell into blank indifference; and all the while, his mind expanded, his ambition took new shapes, which could hardly be satisfied within the sphere his youthful ardour had chosen. But what was he to do? He was a young man of much mental activity, and, above all, gifted with a spirit of contrivance; but then, his faculties would not tell with great effect in any other medium than that of candied sugars, conserves, and pastry. Say what you will about the identity of the reasoning process in all branches of thought, or about the advantage of coming to subjects with a fresh mind, the adjustment of butter to flour, and of heat to pastry, is *not* the best preparation for the office of prime minister; besides, in the present imperfectly-organised state of society, there are social barriers. David could invent delightful things in the way of drop-cakes, and he had the widest views of the sugar department; but in other directions he certainly felt hampered by the want of knowledge and practical skill; and the world is so inconveniently constituted, that the vague consciousness of being a fine fellow is no guarantee of success in any line of business.

This difficulty pressed with some severity on Mr David Faux, even before his apprenticeship was ended. His soul swelled with an impatient sense that he ought to become something very remarkable – that it was quite out of the question for him to put up with a narrow lot as other men did: he scorned the idea that he could accept an average. He was sure there was nothing average about him: even such a person as Mrs Tibbits, the washerwoman, perceived it, and probably had a preference for his linen. At that particular period he was weighing out gingerbread-nuts; but such an anomaly could not continue. No position could be suited to Mr David Faux that was not in the highest degree easy to the flesh and flattering to the spirit. If he had fallen on the present times, and enjoyed the advantages of a Mechanics' Institute, he would certainly have taken to literature and have written reviews; but his education had not been liberal. He had read some novels from the adjoining circulating library, and had even bought the story of 'Inkle and Yarico,' which had made him feel very sorry for poor Mr Inkle; so that his ideas might not have been below a certain mark of the literary calling; but his spelling and diction were too unconventional.

When a man is not adequately appreciated or comfortably placed in his own country, his thoughts naturally turn towards foreign climes; and David's imagination circled round and round the utmost limits of his geographical knowledge, in search of a country where a young gentleman of pasty visage, lipless mouth, and stumpy hair, would be likely to be received with the hospitable enthusiasm which he had a right to expect. Having a general idea of America as a country where the population was chiefly black, it appeared to him the most propitious destination for an emigrant who, to begin with, had the broad and easily recognisable merit of whiteness; and this idea gradually took such strong possession of him that Satan seized the opportunity of suggesting to him that he might emigrate under easier circumstances, if he supplied himself with a little money from his master's till. But that evil spirit, whose understanding, I am convinced, has been much overrated, quite wasted his time on this occasion. David would certainly have liked well to have some of his master's money in his pocket, if he had been sure his master would have been the only man to suffer for it; but he was a cautious youth, and quite determined to run no risks on his own account. So he stayed out his apprenticeship, and committed no act of dishonesty that was at all likely to be discovered, reserving his plan of emigration for a future opportunity. And the circumstances under which he carried it out were in this wise. Having been at home a week or two partaking of the family beans, he had used his leisure in ascertaining a fact which was of considerable importance to him, namely, that his mother had a small sum in guineas painfully saved from her maiden perquisites, and kept in the corner of a drawer where her baby-linen had reposed for the last twenty years – ever since her son David had taken to his feet, with a slight promise of bow-legs which had not been altogether unfulfilled. Mr Faux, senior, had told his son very frankly, that he must not look to being set-up in business by *him:* with seven sons, and one of them a very healthy and well-developed idiot, who consumed a dumpling about eight inches in diameter every day, it was pretty well if they got a hundred apiece at his death. Under these circumstances, what was David to do? It was certainly hard that he should take his mother's money; but he saw no other ready means of getting any, and it was not to be expected that a young man of his merit should put up with inconveniences that could be avoided. Besides, it is not robbery to take property belonging to your mother: she doesn't prosecute you. And David was very well behaved to his mother; he comforted her by speaking highly of himself to her, and assuring her that he never fell into the vices he saw practised by other youths of his own age, and that he was particularly fond of honesty. If his mother would have given him her twenty guineas as a reward of this noble disposition, he really would not have stolen them from her, and it would have been more agreeable to his feelings. Nevertheless, to an active mind like David's, ingenuity is not without its pleasures: it was rather an interesting occupation to become stealthily acquainted with the wards of his mother's simple key (not in the least like Chubb's patent), and to get one that would do its work equally well; and also to arrange a little drama by which he would escape suspicion, and run no risk of forfeiting the prospective hundred at his father's death, which would be convenient in the improbable case of his *not* making a large fortune in the 'Indies.'

First, he spoke freely of his intention to start shortly for Liverpool and take ship for America; a resolution which cost his good mother some pain, for, after Jacob the idiot, there was not one of her sons to whom her heart clung more than to her youngest-born, David. Next, it appeared to him that Sunday afternoon, when everybody was gone to church except Jacob and the cow-boy, was so singularly favourable an opportunity for sons who wanted to appropriate their mothers' guineas, that he half thought it must have been kindly intended by Providence for such purposes. Especially the third Sunday in Lent; because Jacob had been out on one of his occasional wanderings for the last two days; and David, being a timid young man, had a considerable dread and hatred of Jacob, as of a large personage who went about habitually with a pitchfork in his hand.

Nothing could be easier, then, than for David on this Sunday afternoon to decline going to church, on the ground that he was going to tea at Mr Lunn's, whose pretty daughter Sally had been an early flame of his, and, when the church-goers were at a safe distance, to abstract the guineas from their wooden box and slip them into a small canvas bag – nothing easier than to call to the cowboy that he was going, and tell him to keep an eye on the house for fear of Sunday tramps. David thought it would be easy, too, to get to a small thicket and bury his bag in a hole he had already made and covered up under the roots of an old hollow ash, and he had, in fact, found the hole without a moment's difficulty, had uncovered it, and was about gently to drop the bag into it, when the sound of a large body rustling towards him with something like a bellow was such a surprise to David, who, as a gentleman gifted with much contrivance, was naturally only prepared for what he expected, that instead of dropping the bag gently he let it fall so as to make it untwist and vomit forth the shining guineas. In the same moment he looked up and saw his dear brother Jacob close upon him, holding the pitchfork so that the bright smooth prongs were a yard in advance of his own body, and about a foot off David's. (A learned friend, to whom I once narrated this

history, observed that it was David's guilt which made
these prongs formidable, and that the *mens nil conscia
sibi* strips a pitchfork of all terrors. I thought this idea so
valuable, that I obtained his leave to use it on condition of
suppressing his name.) Nevertheless, David did not
entirely lose his presence of mind; for in that case he
would have sunk on the earth or started backward;
whereas he kept his ground and smiled at Jacob, who
nodded his head up and down, and said, 'Hoich, Zavy!'
in a painfully equivocal manner. David's heart was
beating audibly, and if he had had any lips they would
have been pale; but his mental activity, instead of being
paralysed, was stimulated. While he was inwardly
praying (he always prayed when he was much frightened), – 'Oh, save me this once, and I'll never get into
danger again!' – he was thrusting his hand into his
pocket in search of a box of yellow lozenges, which he had
brought with him from Brigford among other delicacies
of the same portable kind, as a means of conciliating
proud beauty, and more particularly the beauty of Miss
Sarah Lunn. Not one of these delicacies had he ever
offered to poor Jacob, for David was not a young man to
waste his jujubes and barley-sugar in giving pleasure to
people from whom he expected nothing. But an idiot
with equivocal intentions and a pitchfork is as well worth
flattering and cajoling as if he were Louis Napoleon. So
David, with a promptitude equal to the occasion, drew
out his box of yellow lozenges, lifted the lid, and per-
formed a pantomime with his mouth and fingers, which
was meant to imply that he was delighted to see his dear
brother Jacob, and seized the opportunity of making him
a small present, which he would find particularly agreeable to the taste. Jacob, you understand, was not an

intense idiot, but within a certain limited range knew
how to choose the good and reject the evil: he took one
lozenge, by way of test, and sucked it as if he had been a
philosopher; then, in as great an ecstasy at its new and
complex savour as Caliban at the taste of Trinculo's wine,
chuckled and stroked this suddenly beneficent brother,
and held out his hand for more; for, except in fits of
anger, Jacob was not ferocious or needlessly predatory.
David's courage half returned, and he left off praying;
pouring a dozen lozenges into Jacob's palm, and trying to
look very fond of him. He congratulated himself that he
had formed the plan of going to see Miss Sally Lunn this
afternoon, and that, as a consequence, he had brought
with him these propitiatory delicacies: he was certainly a
lucky fellow; indeed, it was always likely Providence
should be fonder of him than of other apprentices, and
since he *was* to be interrupted, why, an idiot was pre-
ferable to any other sort of witness. For the first time in his
life, David thought he saw the advantage of idiots.

As for Jacob, he had thrust his pitchfork into the
ground, and had thrown himself down beside it, in thor-
ough abandonment to the unprecedented pleasure of
having five lozenges in his mouth at once, blinking
meanwhile, and making inarticulate sounds of gustative
content. He had not yet given any sign of noticing the
guineas, but in seating himself he had laid his broad right
hand on them, and unconsciously kept it in that position,
absorbed in the sensations of his palate. If he could only
be kept so occupied with the lozenges as not to see the
guineas before David could manage to cover them! That
was David's best hope of safety; for Jacob knew his
mother's guineas; it had been part of their common experience as boys to be allowed to look at these handsome

coins, and rattle them in their box on high days and holidays, and among all Jacob's narrow experiences as to money, this was likely to be the most memorable.

'Here, Jacob,' said David, in an insinuating tone, handing the box to him, 'I'll give 'em all to you. Run! – make haste! – else somebody 'll come and take 'em.'

David, not having studied the psychology of idiots, was not aware that they are not to be wrought upon by imaginative fears. Jacob took the box with his left hand, but saw no necessity for running away. Was ever a promising young man wishing to lay the foundation of his fortune by appropriating his mother's guineas obstructed by such a day-mare as this? But the moment must come when Jacob would move his right hand to draw off the lid of the tin box, and then David would sweep the guineas into the hole with the utmost address and swiftness, and immediately seat himself upon them. Ah, no! It's of no use to have foresight when you are dealing with an idiot: he is not to be calculated upon. Jacob's right hand was given to vague clutching and throwing; it suddenly clutched the guineas as if they had been so many pebbles, and was raised in an attitude which promised to scatter them like seed over a distant bramble, when, from some prompting or other – probably of an unwonted sensation – it paused, descended to Jacob's knee, and opened slowly under the inspection of Jacob's dull eyes. David began to pray again, but immediately desisted – another resource having occurred to him.

'Mother! zinnies!' exclaimed the innocent Jacob. Then, looking at David, he said, interrogatively, 'Box?'

'Hush! hush!' said David, summoning all his ingenuity in this severe strait. 'See, Jacob!' He took the tin box from his brother's hand, and emptied it of the lozenges, returning half of them to Jacob, but secretly keeping the rest in his own hand. Then he held out the empty box, and said, 'Here's the box, Jacob! The box for the guineas!' gently sweeping them from Jacob's palm into the box.

This procedure was not objectionable to Jacob; on the contrary, the guineas clinked so pleasantly as they fell, that he wished for a repetition of the sound, and seizing the box, began to rattle it very gleefully. David, seizing the opportunity, deposited his reserve of lozenges in the ground and hastily swept some earth over them. 'Look, Jacob!' he said, at last. Jacob paused from his clinking, and looked into the hole, while David began to scratch away the earth, as if in doubtful expectation. When the lozenges were laid bare, he took them out one by one, and gave them to Jacob.

'Hush!' he said, in a loud whisper, 'Tell nobody – all for Jacob – hush – sh – sh! Put guineas in the hole – they'll come out like this!' To make the lesson more complete, he took a guinea, and lowering it into the hole, said, 'Put in *so*.' Then, as he took the last lozenge out, he said, 'Come out *so*,' and put the lozenge into Jacob's hospitable mouth.

Jacob turned his head on one side, looked first at his brother and then at the hole, like a reflective monkey, and, finally, laid the box of guineas in the hole with much decision. David made haste to add every one of the stray coins, put on the lid, and covered it well with earth, saying in his most coaxing tone –

'Take 'm out to-morrow, Jacob; all for Jacob! Hush – sh – sh!'

Jacob, to whom this once indifferent brother had all at once become a sort of sweet-tasted fetish, stroked David's best coat with his adhesive fingers, and then hugged him with an accompaniment of that mingled chuckling and gurgling by which he was accustomed to express the milder passions. But if he had chosen to bite a small morsel out of his beneficent brother's cheek, David would have been obliged to bear it.

And here I must pause, to point out to you the short-sightedness of human contrivance. This ingenious young man, Mr David Faux, thought he had achieved a triumph of cunning when he had associated himself in his brother's rudimentary mind with the flavour of yellow lozenges. But he had yet to learn that it is a dreadful thing to make an idiot fond of you, when you yourself are not of an affectionate disposition: especially an idiot with a pitchfork – obviously a difficult friend to shake off by rough usage.

It may seem to you rather a blundering contrivance for a clever young man to bury the guineas. But, if everything had turned out as David had calculated, you would have seen that his plan was worthy of his talents. The guineas would have lain safely in the earth while the theft was discovered, and David, with the calm of conscious innocence, would have lingered at home, reluctant to say good-bye to his dear mother while she was in grief about her guineas; till at length, on the eve of his departure, he would have disinterred them in the strictest privacy, and carried them on his own person without inconvenience. But David, you perceive, had reckoned without his host, or, to speak more precisely, without his idiot brother – an item of so uncertain and fluctuating a character, that I doubt whether he would not have puzzled the astute heroes of M. de Balzac, whose foresight is so remarkably at home in the future.

It was clear to David now that he had only one alternative before him: he must either renounce the guineas,
by quietly putting them back in his mother's drawer
(a course not unattended with difficulty); or he must
leave more than a suspicion behind him, by departing
early the next morning without giving notice, and with
the guineas in his pocket. For if he gave notice that he
was going, his mother, he knew, would insist on fetching
from her box of guineas the three she had always promised him as his share; indeed, in his original plan, he
had counted on this as a means by which the theft would
be discovered under circumstances that would themselves
speak for his innocence; but now, as I need hardly explain,
that well-combined plan was completely frustrated. Even
if David could have bribed Jacob with perpetual lozenges, an idiot's secrecy is itself betrayal. He dared not
even go to tea at Mr Lunn's, for in that case he would have
lost sight of Jacob, who, in his impatience for the crop of
lozenges, might scratch up the box again while he was
absent, and carry it home – depriving him at once of
reputation and guineas. No! he must think of nothing
all the rest of this day, but of coaxing Jacob and keeping him out of mischief. It was a fatiguing and anxious
evening to David; nevertheless, he dared not go to sleep
without tying a piece of string to his thumb and great toe,
to secure his frequent waking; for he meant to be up with
the first peep of dawn, and be far out of reach before
breakfast-time. His father, he thought, would certainly
cut him off with a shilling; but what then? Such a striking
young man as he would be sure to be well received in the
West Indies: in foreign countries there are always open-
ings – even for cats. It was probable that some Princess
Yarico would want him to marry her, and make him pres-

ents of very large jewels beforehand; after which, he needn't marry her unless he liked. David had made up his mind not to steal any more, even from people who were fond of him: it was an unpleasant way of making your fortune in a world where you were likely to be surprised in the act by brothers. Such alarms did not agree with David's constitution, and he had felt so much nausea this evening that no doubt his liver was affected. Besides, he would have been greatly hurt not to be thought well of in the world: he always meant to make a figure, and be thought worthy of the best seats and the best morsels.

Ruminating to this effect on the brilliant future in reserve for him, David by the help of his check-string kept himself on the alert to seize the time of earliest dawn for his rising and departure. His brothers, of course, were early risers, but he should anticipate them by at least an hour and a half, and the little room which he had to himself as only an occasional visitor, had its window over the horse-block, so that he could slip out through the window without the least difficulty. Jacob, the horrible Jacob, had an awkward trick of getting up before everybody else, to stem his hunger by emptying the milk-bowl that was 'duly set' for him; but of late he had taken to sleeping in the hay-loft, and if he came into the house, it would be on the opposite side to that from which David was making his exit. There was no need to think of Jacob; yet David was liberal enough to bestow a curse on him – it was the only thing he ever did bestow gratuitously. His small bundle of clothes was ready packed, and he was soon treading lightly on the steps of the horse-block, soon walking at a smart pace across the fields towards the thicket. It would take him no more than two minutes to get out the box; he could make out the tree it was under by the pale strip where the bark was off, although the dawning light was rather dimmer in the thicket. But what, in the name of – burnt pastry – was that large body with a staff planted beside it, close at the foot of the ash-tree? David paused, not to make up his mind as to the nature of the apparition – he had not the happiness of doubting for a moment that the staff was Jacob's pitch-fork – but to gather the self-command necessary for addressing his brother with a sufficiently honeyed accent. Jacob was absorbed in scratching up the earth, and had not heard David's approach.

'I say, Jacob,' said David in a loud whisper, just as the tin box was lifted out of the hole.

Jacob looked up, and discerning his sweet-flavoured brother, nodded and grinned in the dim light in a way that made him seem to David like a triumphant demon. If he had been of an impetuous disposition, he would have snatched the pitchfork from the ground and impaled this fraternal demon. But David was by no means impetuous; he was a young man greatly given to calculate consequences, a habit which has been held to be the foundation of virtue. But somehow it had not pre-cisely that effect in David: he calculated whether an action would harm himself, or whether it would only harm other people. In the former case he was very timid about satisfying his immediate desires, but in the latter he would risk the result with much courage.

'Give it *me*, Jacob,' he said, stooping down and patting his brother. 'Let us see.'

Jacob, finding the lid rather tight, gave the box to his brother in perfect faith. David raised the lid, and shook his head, while Jacob put his finger in and took out a guinea to taste whether the metamorphosis into lozenges was complete and satisfactory.

'No, Jacob; too soon, too soon,' said David, when the guinea had been tasted. 'Give it me; we'll go and bury it somewhere else; we'll put it in yonder,' he added, pointing vaguely toward the distance.

David screwed on the lid, while Jacob, looking grave, rose and grasped his pitchfork. Then, seeing David's bundle, he snatched it, like a too officious Newfoundland, stuck his pitchfork into it and carried it over his shoulder in triumph as he accompanied David and the box out of the thicket.

What on earth was David to do? It would have been easy to frown at Jacob, and kick him, and order him to get away; but David dared as soon have kicked the bull. Jacob was quiet as long as he was treated indulgently; but on the slightest show of anger, he became unmanageable, and was liable to fits of fury which would have made him formidable even without his pitchfork. There was no mastery to be obtained over him except by kindness or guile. David tried guile.

'Go, Jacob,' he said, when they were out of the thicket – pointing towards the house as he spoke; 'go and fetch me a spade – a spade. But give *me* the bundle,' he added, trying to reach it from the fork, where it hung high above Jacob's tall shoulder.

But Jacob showed as much alacrity in obeying as a wasp shows in leaving a sugar-basin. Near David, he felt himself in the vicinity of lozenges: he chuckled and rubbed his brother's back, brandishing the bundle higher out of reach. David, with an inward groan, changed his tactics, and walked on as fast as he could. It was not safe to linger. Jacob would get tired of following him, or, at all events, could be eluded. If they could once get to the distant highroad, a coach would overtake them, David would mount it, having previously by some ingenious means secured his bundle, and then Jacob might howl and flourish his pitchfork as much as he liked. Meanwhile he was under the fatal necessity of being very kind to this ogre, and of providing a large breakfast for him when they stopped at a roadside inn. It was already three hours since they had started, and David was tired. Would no coach be coming up soon? he inquired. No coach for the next two hours. But there was a carrier's cart to come immediately, on its way to the next town. If he could slip out, even leaving his bundle behind, and get into the cart without Jacob! But there was a new obstacle. Jacob had recently discovered a remnant of sugar-candy in one of his brother's tail-pockets; and, since then, had cautiously kept his hold on that limb of the garment, perhaps with an expectation that there would be a further develop-ment of sugar-candy after a longer or shorter interval. Now every one who has worn a coat will understand the sensibilities that must keep a man from starting away in a hurry when there is a grasp on his coat-tail. David looked forward to being well received among strangers, but it might make a difference if he had only one tail to his coat.

He felt himself in a cold perspiration. He could walk no more: he must get into the cart and let Jacob get in with him. Presently a cheering idea occurred to him: after so large a breakfast, Jacob would be sure to go to sleep in the cart; you see at once that David meant to seize his bundle, jump out, and be free. His expectation was partly fulfil-led: Jacob did go to sleep in the cart, but it was in a pecu-liar attitude – it was with his arms tightly fastened round his dear brother's body; and if ever David attempted to

move, the grasp tightened with the force of an affectionate boa-constrictor.

'Th' innicent's fond on you,' observed the carrier,
thinking that David was probably an amiable brother,
and wishing to pay him a compliment.

David groaned. The ways of thieving were not ways of
pleasantness. Oh, why had he an idiot brother? Or why,
in general, was the world so constituted that a man could
not take his mother's guineas comfortably? David
became grimly speculative.

Copious dinner at noon for Jacob; but little dinner,
because little appetite, for David. Instead of eating, he
plied Jacob with beer; for through this liberality he
descried a hope. Jacob fell into a dead sleep, at last, *without* having his arms round David, who paid the reckon-
ing, took his bundle, and walked off. In another half-
hour he was on the coach on his way to Liverpool, smiling
the smile of the triumphant wicked. He was rid of Jacob –
he was bound for the Indies, where a gullible princess
awaited him. He would never steal any more, but there
would be no need; he would show himself so deserving,
that people would make him presents freely. He must
give up the notion of his father's legacy; but it was not
likely he would ever want that trifle; and even if he did –
why, it was a compensation to think that in being for ever
divided from his family he was divided from Jacob, more
terrible than Gorgon or Demogorgon to David's timid
green eyes. Thank heaven, he should never see Jacob any
more!

CHAPTER 2

It was nearly six years after the departure of Mr David Faux for the West Indies, that the vacant shop in the market-place at Grimworth was understood to have been let to the stranger with a sallow complexion and a buff cravat, whose first appearance had caused some excitement in the bar of the Woolpack, where he had called to wait for the coach.

Grimworth, to a discerning eye, was a good place to set up shopkeeping in. There was no competition in it at present; the Church-people had their own grocer and draper; the Dissenters had theirs; and the two or three butchers found a ready market for their joints without strict reference to religious persuasion – except that the rector's wife had given a general order for the veal sweet-breads and the mutton kidneys, while Mr Rodd, the Baptist minister, had requested that, so far as was compatible with the fair accommodation of other customers, the sheep's trotters might be reserved for him. And it was likely to be a growing place, for the trustees of Mr Zephaniah Crypt's Charity, under the stimulus of a late visitation by commissioners, were beginning to apply long-accumulating funds to the rebuilding of the Yellow Coat School, which was henceforth to be carried forward on a greatly-extended scale, the testator having left no restrictions concerning the curriculum, but only concerning the coat.

The shopkeepers at Grimworth were by no means

unanimous as to the advantages promised by this prospect of increased population and trading, being substantial men, who liked doing a quiet business in which they were sure of their customers, and could calculate their returns to a nicety. Hitherto, it had been held a point of honour by the families in Grimworth parish, to buy their sugar and their flannel at the shops where their fathers and mothers had bought before them; but, if newcomers were to bring in the system of neck-and-neck trading, and solicit feminine eyes by gown-pieces laid in fan-like folds, and surmounted by artificial flowers, giving them a factitious charm (for on what human figure would a gown sit like a fan, or what female head was like a bunch of China-asters?), or, if new grocers were to fill their windows with mountains of currants and sugar, made seductive by contrast and tickets, – what security was there for Grimworth, that a vagrant spirit in shopping, once introduced, would not in the end carry the most important families to the larger market town of Cattleton, where, business being done on a system of small profits and quick returns, the fashions were of the freshest, and goods of all kinds might be bought at an advantage?

With this view of the times predominant among the tradespeople at Grimworth, their uncertainty concerning the nature of the business which the sallow-complexioned stranger was about to set up in the vacant shop, naturally gave some additional strength to the fears of the less sanguine. If he was going to sell drapery, it was probable that a pale-faced fellow like that would deal in showy and inferior articles – printed cottons and muslins which would leave their dye in the wash-tube, jobbed linen full of knots, and flannel that would soon look like gauze. If grocery, then it was to be hoped that no mother of a family would trust the teas of an untried grocer. Such things had been known in some parishes as tradesmen going about canvassing for custom with cards in their pockets: when people came from nobody knew where, there was no knowing what they might do. It was a thousand pities that Mr Moffat, the auctioneer and broker, had died without leaving anybody to follow him in the business, and Mrs Cleve's trustee ought to have known better than to let a shop to a stranger. Even the discovery that ovens were being put up on the premises, and that the shop was, in fact, being fitted up for a confectioner and pastry-cook's business, hitherto unknown in Grimworth, did not quite suffice to turn the scale in the new-comer's favour, though the landlady at the Woolpack defended him warmly, said he seemed to be a very clever young man, and from what she could make out, came of a very good family; indeed, was most likely a good many people's betters.

It certainly made a blaze of light and colour, almost as if a rainbow had suddenly descended into the market-place, when, one fine morning, the shutters were taken down from the new shop, and the two windows displayed their decorations. On one side, there were the variegated tints of collared and marbled meats, set off by bright green leaves, the pale brown of glazed pies, the rich tones of sauces and bottled fruits enclosed in their veil of glass – altogether a sight to bring tears into the eyes of a Dutch painter; and on the other, there was a predominance of the more delicate hues of pink, and white, and yellow, and buff, in the abundant lozenges, candies, sweet biscuits and icings, which to the eyes of a bilious person might easily have been blended into a faëry landscape in Turner's latest style. What a sight to dawn upon the eyes of Grimworth children! They almost forgot to go to their dinner that day, their appetites being preoccupied with imaginary sugar-plums; and I think even Punch, setting up his tabernacle in the market-place, would not have succeeded in drawing them away from those shop-windows, where they stood according to gradations of size and strength, the biggest and strongest being nearest the window, and the little ones in the outermost rows lifting wide-open eyes and mouths towards the upper tier of jars, like small birds at meal-time.

The elder inhabitants pished and pshawed a little at the folly of the new shopkeeper in venturing on such an outlay in goods that would not keep; to be sure, Christmas was coming, but what housewife in Grimworth would not think shame to furnish forth her table with articles that were not home-cooked? No, no. Mr Edward Freely, as he called himself, was deceived, if he thought Grimworth money was to flow into his pockets on such terms.

Edward Freely was the name that shone in gilt letters on a mazarine ground over the doorplace of the new shop – a generous-sounding name, that might have belonged to the open-hearted, improvident hero of an old comedy, who would have delighted in raining sugared almonds, like a new manna-gift, among that small generation outside the windows. But Mr Edward Freely was a man whose impulses were kept in due subordination: he held that the desire for sweets and pastry must only be satisfied in a direct ratio with the power of paying for them. If the smallest child in Grimworth would go to him with a halfpenny in its tiny fist, he would, after

ringing the halfpenny, deliver a just equivalent in 'rock.'
He was not a man to cheat even the smallest child – he
often said so, observing at the same time that he loved
honesty, and also that he was very tender-hearted,
though he didn't show his feelings as some people did.

Either in reward of such virtue, or according to some
more hidden law of sequence, Mr Freely's business, in
spite of prejudice, started under favourable auspices. For
Mrs Chaloner, the rector's wife, was among the earliest
customers at the shop, thinking it only right to encourage
a new parishioner who had made a decorous appearance
at church; and she found Mr Freely a most civil, obliging
young man, and intelligent to a surprising degree for a
confectioner; well-principled, too, for in giving her
useful hints about choosing sugars he had thrown much
light on the dishonesty of other tradesmen. Moreover, he
had been in the West Indies, and had seen the very estate
which had been her poor grandfather's property; and he
said the missionaries were the only cause of the negro's
discontent – an observing young man, evidently. Mrs
Chaloner ordered wine-biscuits and olives, and gave Mr
Freely to understand that she should find his shop a great
convenience. So did the doctor's wife, and so did Mrs
Gate, at the large carding-mill, who, having high con-
nections frequently visiting her, might be expected to
have a large consumption of ratafias and macaroons.

The less aristocratic matrons of Grimworth seemed
likely at first to justify their husbands' confidence that
they would never pay a percentage of profits on drop-
cakes, instead of making their own, or get up a hollow
show of liberal housekeeping by purchasing slices of collared meat when a neighbour came in for supper. But it is
my task to narrate the gradual corruption of Grimworth

manners from their primitive simplicity – a melancholy task, if it were not cheered by the prospect of the fine peripateia or downfall by which the progress of the corruption was ultimately checked.

It was young Mrs Steene, the veterinary surgeon's wife, who first gave way to temptation. I fear she had been rather over-educated for her station in life, for she knew by heart many passages in 'Lalla Rookh,' the 'Corsair,' and the 'Siege of Corinth,' which had given her a distaste for domestic occupations, and caused her a withering disappointment at the discovery that Mr Steene, since his marriage, had lost all interest in the 'bulbul,' openly preferred discussing the nature of spavin with a coarse neighbour, and was angry if the pudding turned out watery – indeed, was simply a top-booted 'vet.,' who came in hungry at dinner-time; and not in the least like a nobleman turned Corsair out of pure scorn for his race, or like a renegade with a turban and crescent, unless it were in the irritability of his temper. And scorn is such a very different thing in top-boots!

This brutal man had invited a supper-party for Christmas eve, when he would expect to see mince-pies on the table. Mrs Steene had prepared her mince-meat, and had devoted much butter, fine flour, and labour, to the making of a batch of pies in the morning; but they proved to be so very heavy when they came out of the oven, that she could only think with trembling of the moment when her husband should catch sight of them on the supper-table. He would storm at her, she was certain; and before all the company; and then she should never help crying; it was so dreadful to think she had come to that, after the bulbul and everything! Suddenly the thought darted through her mind that *this once* she might send for a dish of mince-pies from Freely's: she knew he had some. But what was to become of the eighteen heavy mince-pies? Oh, it was of no use thinking about that; it was very expensive – indeed, making mince-pies at all was a great expense, when they were not sure to turn out well: it would be much better to buy them ready-made. You paid a little more for them, but there was no risk of waste.

Such was the sophistry with which this misguided young woman – enough. Mrs Steene sent for the mince-pies, and, I am grieved to add, garbled her household accounts in order to conceal the fact from her husband. This was the second step in a downward course, all owing to a young woman's being out of harmony with her circumstances, yearning after renegades and bulbuls, and being subject to claims from a veterinary surgeon fond of mince-pies. The third step was to harden herself by telling the fact of the bought mince-pies to her intimate friend Mrs Mole, who had already guessed it, and who subsequently encouraged herself in buying a mould of jelly, instead of exerting her own skill, by the reflection that 'other people' did the same sort of thing. The infection spread; soon there was a party or clique in Grimworth on the side of 'buying at Freely's;' and many husbands, kept for some time in the dark on this point, innocently swallowed at two mouthfuls a tart on which they were paying a profit of a hundred per cent, and as innocently encouraged a fatal disingenuousness in the partners of their bosoms by praising the pastry. Others, more keen-sighted, winked at the too frequent presentation on washing-days, and at impromptu suppers, of superior spiced-beef, which flattered their palates more than the cold remnants they had formerly been contented with. Every housewife who had once 'bought at

Freely's' felt a secret joy when she detected a similar
perversion in her neighbour's practice, and soon only two
or three old-fashioned mistresses of families held out in
the protest against the growing demoralisation, saying to
their neighbours who came to sup with them, 'I can't
offer you Freely's beef, or Freely's cheese-cakes; everything in our house is home-made; I'm afraid you'll
hardly have any appetite for our plain pastry.' The doctor, whose cook was not satisfactory, the curate, who kept
no cook, and the mining agent, who was a great *bon
vivant*, even began to rely on Freely for the greater part of
their dinner, when they wished to give an entertainment
of some brilliancy. In short, the business of manufactur-
ing the more fanciful viands was fast passing out of the
hands of maids and matrons in private families, and was
becoming the work of a special commercial organ.

I am not ignorant that this sort of thing is called the
inevitable course of civilisation, division of labour, and
so forth, and that the maids and matrons may be said to
have had their hands set free from cookery to add to the
wealth of society in some other way. Only it happened at
Grimworth, which, to be sure, was a low place, that the
maids and matrons could do nothing with their hands at
all better than cooking; not even those who had always
made heavy cakes and leathery pastry. And so it came to
pass, that the progress of civilisation at Grimworth was
not otherwise apparent than in the impoverishment of
men, the gossiping idleness of women, and the height-
ening prosperity of Mr Edward Freely.

The Yellow Coat School was a double source of profit
to the calculating confectioner; for he opened an eating-
room for the superior workmen employed on the new
school, and he accommodated the pupils at the old

school by giving great attention to the fancy-sugar department. When I think of the sweet-tasted swans and other ingenious white shapes crunched by the small teeth of that rising generation, I am glad to remember that a certain amount of calcareous food has been held good for young creatures whose bones are not quite formed; for I have observed these delicacies to have an inorganic flavour which would have recommended them greatly to that young lady of the 'Spectator's' acquaintance who habitually made her dessert on the stems of tobacco-pipes.

As for the confectioner himself, he made his way gradually into Grimworth homes, as his commodities did, in spite of some initial repugnance. Somehow or other, his reception as a guest seemed a thing that required justifying, like the purchasing of his pastry. In the first place, he was a stranger, and therefore open to suspicion; secondly, the confectionery business was so entirely new at Grimworth, that its place in the scale of rank had not been distinctly ascertained. There was no doubt about drapers and grocers, when they came of good old Grimworth families, like Mr Luff and Mr Prettyman: they visited with the Palfreys, who farmed their own land, played many a game at whist with the doctor, and condescended a little towards the timber-merchant, who had lately taken to the coal-trade also, and had got new furniture; but whether a confectioner should be admitted to this higher level of respectability, or should be understood to find his associates among butchers and bakers, was a new question on which tradition threw no light. His being a bachelor was in his favour, and would perhaps have been enough to turn the scale, even if Mr Edward Freely's other personal pretensions had been of

an entirely insignificant cast. But so far from this, it very
soon appeared that he was a remarkable young man, who
had been in the West Indies, and had seen many won-
ders by sea and land, so that he could charm the ears of
Grimworth Desdemonas with stories of strange fishes,
especially sharks, which he had stabbed in the nick of
time by bravely plunging overboard just as the monster
was turning on his side to devour the cook's mate; of
terrible fevers which he had undergone in a land where
the wind blows from all quarters at once; of rounds of
toast cut straight from the bread-fruit trees; of toes bitten
off by land-crabs; of large honours that had been offered
to him as a man who knew what was what, and was
therefore particularly needed in a tropical climate; and of
a Creole heiress who had wept bitterly at his departure.
Such conversational talents as these, we know, will overcome disadvantages of complexion; and young Towers,
whose cheeks were of the finest pink, set off by a fringe of
dark whisker, was quite eclipsed by the presence of the
sallow Mr Freely. So exceptional a confectioner elevated
his business, and might well begin to make disengaged
hearts flutter a little.

Fathers and mothers were naturally more slow and
cautious in their recognition of the new-comer's merits.

'He's an amusing fellow,' said Mr Prettyman, the
highly respectable grocer. (Mrs Prettyman was a Miss
Fothergill, and her sister had married a London mercer.)
'He's an amusing fellow; and I've no objection to his
making one at the Oyster Club; but he's a bit too fond of
riding the high horse. He's uncommonly knowing, I'll
allow; but how came he to go to the Indies? I should like
that answered. It's unnatural in a confectioner. I'm not
fond of people that have been beyond seas, if they can't

give a good account how they happened to go. When folks go so far off, it's because they've got little credit nearer home – that's my opinion. However, he's got some good rum; but I don't want to be hand and glove with him, for all that.'

It was this kind of dim suspicion which beclouded the view of Mr Freely's qualities in the maturer minds of Grimworth through the early months of his residence there. But when the confectioner ceased to be a novelty, the suspicions also ceased to be novel, and people got tired of hinting at them, especially as they seemed to be refuted by his advancing prosperity and importance. Mr Freely was becoming a person of influence in the parish; he was found useful as an overseer of the poor, having great firmness in enduring other people's pain, which firmness, he said, was due to his great benevolence; he always did what was good for people in the end. Mr Chaloner had even selected him as clergyman's church-warden, for he was a very handy man, and much more of Mr Chaloner's opinion in everything about church business than the older parishioners. Mr Freely was a very regular churchman, but at the Oyster Club he was some-times a little free in his conversation, more than hinting at a life of Sultanic self-indulgence which he had passed in the West Indies, shaking his head now and then and smiling rather bitterly, as men are wont to do when they intimate that they have become a little too wise to be instructed about a world which has long been flat and stale to them.

For some time he was quite general in his attentions to the fair sex, combining the gallantries of a lady's man with a severity of criticism on the person and manners of absent belles, which tended rather to stimulate in the feminine breast the desire to conquer the approval of so fastidious a judge. Nothing short of the very best in the department of female charms and virtues could suffice to kindle the ardour of Mr Edward Freely, who had become familiar with the most luxuriant and dazzling beauty in the West Indies. It may seem incredible that a confectioner should have ideas and conversation so much resembling those to be met with in a higher walk of life, but it must be remembered that he had not merely travelled, he had also bow-legs and a sallow, small-featured visage, so that nature herself had stamped him for a fastidious connoisseur of the fair sex.

At last, however, it seemed clear that Cupid had found a sharper arrow than usual, and that Mr Freely's heart was pierced. It was the general talk among the young people at Grimworth. But was it really love? and not rather ambition? Miss Fullilove, the timber-merchant's daughter, was quite sure that if *she* were Miss Penny Palfrey, she would be cautious; it was not a good sign when men looked so much above themselves for a wife. For it was no less a person than Miss Penelope Palfrey, second daughter of the Mr Palfrey who farmed his own land, that had attracted Mr Freely's peculiar regard, and conquered his fastidiousness; and no wonder; for the Ideal, as exhibited in the finest waxwork, was perhaps never so closely approached by the Real as in the person of the pretty Penelope. Her yellowish flaxen hair did not curl naturally, I admit, but its bright crisp ringlets were such smooth, perfect miniature tubes, that you would have longed to pass your little finger through them, and feel their soft elasticity. She wore them in a crop, for in those days, when society was in a healthier state, young ladies wore crops long after they were twenty, and Penelope was not yet nineteen. Like the waxen ideal, she had round blue eyes, and round nostrils in her little nose, and teeth such as the ideal would be seen to have, if it ever showed them. Altogether, she was a small, round thing, as neat as a pink and white double daisy, and as guileless; for I hope it does not argue guile in a pretty damsel of nineteen, to think that she should like to have a beau and be 'engaged,' when her elder sister had already been in that position a year and a half. To be sure, there was young Towers always coming to the house; but Penny felt convinced he only came to see her brother, for he never had anything to say to her, and never offered her his arm, and was as awkward and silent as possible.

It is not unlikely that Mr Freely had early been smitten by Penny's charms, as brought under his observation at church, but he had to make his way in society a little before he could come into nearer contact with them; and even after he was well received in Grimworth families, it was a long while before he could converse with Penny otherwise than in an incidental meeting at Mr Luff's. It was not so easy to get invited to Long Meadows, the residence of the Palfreys; for though Mr Palfrey had been losing money of late years, not being able quite to recover his feet after the terrible murrain which forced him to borrow, his family were far from considering themselves on the same level even as the old-established tradespeople with whom they visited. The greatest people, even kings and queens, must visit with somebody, and the equals of the great are scarce. They were especially scarce at Grimworth, which, as I have before observed, was a low parish, mentioned with the most scornful brevity in gazetteers. Even the great people there were far behind those of their own standing

in other parts of this realm. Mr Palfrey's farmyard
doors had the paint all worn off them, and the front
garden walks had long been merged in a general weedi-
ness. Still, his father had been called Squire Palfrey,
and had been respected by the last Grimworth generation as a man who could afford to drink too much in his
own house.

Pretty Penny was not blind to the fact that Mr Freely
admired her, and she felt sure that it was he who had sent
her a beautiful valentine; but her sister seemed to think
so lightly of him (all young ladies think lightly of the
gentlemen to whom they are not engaged), that Penny
never dared mention him, and trembled and blushed
whenever they met him, thinking of the valentine, which
was very strong in its expressions, and which she felt
guilty of knowing by heart. A man who had been to the
Indies, and knew the sea so well, seemed to her a sort of
public character, almost like Robinson Crusoe or Captain
Cook; and Penny had always wished her husband to be a
remarkable personage, likely to be put in Mangnall's
Questions, with which register of the immortals she had
become acquainted during her one year at a boarding-
school. Only it seemed strange that a remarkable man
should be a confectioner and pastry-cook, and this
anomaly quite disturbed Penny's dreams. Her brothers,
she knew, laughed at men who couldn't sit on horseback
well, and called them tailors; but her brothers were very
rough, and were quite without that power of anecdote
which made Mr Freely such a delightful companion. He
was a very good man, she thought, for she had heard him
say at Mr Luff's, one day, that he always wished to do his
duty in whatever state of life he might be placed; and he
knew a great deal of poetry, for one day he had repeated a

verse of a song. She wondered if he had made the words
of the valentine! – it ended in this way: –

'Without thee, it is pain to live,
But with thee, it were sweet to die.'

Poor Mr Freely! her father would very likely
object – she felt sure he would, for he always called Mr
Freely 'that sugar-plum fellow.' Oh, it was very cruel,
when true love was crossed in that way, and all because
Mr Freely was a confectioner: well, Penny would be true
to him, for all that, and since his being a confectioner
gave her an opportunity of showing her faithfulness, she
was glad of it. Edward Freely was a pretty name, much
better than John Towers. Young Towers had offered her
a rose out of his button-hole the other day, blushing very
much; but she refused it, and thought with delight how
much Mr Freely would be comforted if he knew her
firmness of mind.

Poor little Penny! the days were so very long among the
daisies on a grazing farm, and thought is so active – how
was it possible that the inward drama should not get the
start of the outward? I have known young ladies, much
better educated, and with an outward world diversified
by instructive lectures, to say nothing of literature and
highly-developed fancy-work, who have spun a cocoon of
visionary joys and sorrows for themselves, just as Penny
did. Her elder sister Letitia, who had a prouder style of
beauty, and a more worldly ambition, was engaged to a
wool-factor, who came all the way from Cattelton to see
her; and everybody knows that a wool-factor takes a very
high rank, sometimes driving a double-bodied gig.
Letty's notions got higher every day, and Penny never
dared to speak of her cherished griefs to her lofty

sister – never dared to propose that they should call at Mr Freely's to buy liquorice, though she had prepared for such an incident by mentioning a slight sore throat. So she had to pass the shop on the other side of the market-place, and reflect, with a suppressed sigh, that behind those pink and white jars somebody was thinking of her tenderly, unconscious of the small space that divided her from him.

And it was quite true that, when business permitted, Mr Freely thought a great deal of Penny. He thought her prettiness comparable to the loveliest things in confectionery; he judged her to be of submissive temper – likely to wait upon him as well as if she had been a negress, and to be silently terrified when his liver made him irritable; and he considered the Palfrey family quite the best in the parish, possessing marriageable daughters. On the whole, he thought her worthy to become Mrs Edward Freely, and all the more so, because it would probably require some ingenuity to win her. Mr Palfrey was capable of horse-whipping a too rash pretender to his daughter's hand; and, moreover, he had three tall sons: it was clear that a suitor would be at a disadvantage with such a family, unless travel and natural acumen had given him a countervailing power of contrivance. And the first idea that occurred to him in the matter was, that Mr Palfrey would object less if he knew that the Freelys were a much higher family than his own. It had been foolish modesty in him hitherto to conceal the fact that a branch of the Freelys held a manor in Yorkshire, and to shut up the portrait of his great uncle the admiral, instead of hanging it up where a family portrait should be hung – over the mantelpiece in the parlour. Admiral Freely, K.C.B., once placed in this conspicuous position, was seen to have had one arm only, and one eye, – in these points resembling the heroic Nelson, – while a certain pallid insignificance of feature confirmed the relationship between himself and his grand-nephew.

Next, Mr Freely was seized with an irrepressible ambition to possess Mrs Palfrey's receipt for brawn, hers being pronounced on all hands to be superior to his own – as he informed her in a very flattering letter carried by his errand-boy. Now Mrs Palfrey, like other geniuses, wrought by instinct rather than by rule, and possessed no receipts, – indeed, despised all people who used them, observing that people who pickled by book, must pickle by weights and measures, and such nonsense; as for herself, her weights and measures were the tip of her finger and the tip of her tongue, and if you went nearer, why, of course, for dry goods like flour and spice, you went by handfuls and pinches, and for wet, there was a middle-sized jug – quite the best thing whether for much or little, because you might know how much a teacupful was if you'd got any use of your senses, and you might be sure it would take five middle-sized jugs to make a gallon. Knowledge of this kind is like Titian's colouring, difficult to communicate; and as Mrs Palfrey, once remarkably handsome, had now become rather stout and asthmatical, and scarcely ever left home, her oral teaching could hardly be given anywhere except at Long Meadows. Even a matron is not insusceptible to flattery, and the prospect of a visitor whose great object would be to listen to her conversation, was not without its charms to Mrs Palfrey. Since there was no receipt to be sent in reply to Mr Freely's humble request, she called on her more docile daughter, Penny, to write a note, telling him that her mother would be glad to see him and talk with him on brawn, any day that he could call at Long Meadows. Penny obeyed with a trembling hand, thinking how wonderfully things came about in this world.

In this way, Mr Freely got himself introduced into the home of the Palfreys, and notwithstanding a tendency in the male part of the family to jeer at him a little as 'peaky' and bow-legged, he presently established his position as an accepted and frequent guest. Young Towers looked at him with increasing disgust when they met at the house on a Sunday, and secretly longed to try his ferret upon him, as a piece of vermin which that valuable animal would be likely to tackle with unhesitating vigour. But – so blind sometimes are parents – neither Mr nor Mrs Palfrey suspected that Penny would have anything to say to a tradesman of questionable rank whose youthful bloom was much withered. Young Towers, they thought, had an eye to her, and *that* was likely enough to be a match some day; but Penny was a child at present. And all the while Penny was imagining the circumstances under which Mr Freely would make her an offer: perhaps down by the row of damson-trees, when they were in the garden before tea; perhaps by letter – in which case, how would the letter begin? 'Dearest Penelope?' or 'Mr dear Miss Penelope?' or straight off, without dear anything, as seemed the most natural when people were embarrassed? But, however he might make the offer, she would not accept it without her father's consent: she would always be true to Mr Freely, but she would not disobey her father. For Penny was a good girl, though some of her female friends were afterwards of opinion that it spoke ill for her not to have felt an instinctive repugnance to Mr Freely.

But he was cautious, and wished to be quite sure of the ground he trod on. His views in marriage were not entirely sentimental, but were as duly mingled with considerations of what would be advantageous to a man in his position, as if he had had a very large amount of money spent on his education. He was not a man to fall in love in the wrong place; and so, he applied himself quite as much to conciliate the favour of the parents, as to secure the attachment of Penny. Mrs Palfrey had not been inaccessible to flattery, and her husband, being also of mortal mould, would not, it might be hoped, be proof against rum – that very fine Jamaica rum of which Mr Freely expected always to have a supply sent him from Jamaica. It was not easy to get Mr Palfrey into the parlour behind the shop, where a mild back-street light fell on the features of the heroic admiral; but by getting hold of him rather late one evening as he was about to return home from Grimworth, the aspiring lover succeeded in persuading him to sup on some collared beef which, after Mrs Palfrey's brawn, he would find the very best of cold eating.

From that hour Mr Freely felt sure of success: being in privacy with an estimable man old enough to be his father, and being rather lonely in the world, it was natural he should unbosom himself a little on subjects which he could not speak of in a mixed circle – especially concerning his expectations from his uncle in Jamaica, who had no children, and loved his nephew Edward better than any one else in the world, though he had been so hurt at his leaving Jamaica, that he had threatened to cut him off with a shilling. However, he had since written to state his full forgiveness, and though he was an eccentric old gentleman and could not bear to give away money during his life, Mr Edward Freely could show Mr Palfrey the letter which declared, plainly enough, who would be the affectionate uncle's heir. Mr Palfrey actually saw the letter, and could not help admiring the spirit of the nephew who declared that such brilliant hopes as these made no difference to his conduct; he should work at his humble business and make his modest fortune at it all the same. If the Jamaica estate was to come to him – well and good. It was nothing very surprising for one of the Freely family to have an estate left him, considering the lands that family had possessed in time gone by, – nay possessed in the Northumberland branch. Would not Mr Palfrey take another glass of rum? and also look at the last year's balance of the accounts? Mr Freely was a man who cared to possess personal virtues, and did not pique himself on his family, though some men would.

We know how easily the great Leviathan may be led, when once there is a hook in his nose or a bridle in his jaws. Mr Palfrey was a large man, but, like Leviathan's, his bulk went against him when once he had taken a turning. He was not a mercurial man, who easily changed his point of view. Enough. Before two months were over, he had given his consent to Mr Freely's marriage with his daughter Penny, and having hit on a formula by which he could justify it, fenced off all doubts and objections, his own included. The formula was this: 'I'm not a man to put my head up an entry before I know where it leads.'

Little Penny was very proud and fluttering, but hardly so happy as she expected to be in an engagement. She wondered if young Towers cared much about it, for he had not been to the house lately, and her sister and brothers were rather inclined to sneer than to sympathise. Grimworth rang with the news. All men extolled

Mr Freely's good fortune; while the women, with the tender solicitude characteristic of the sex, wished the marriage might turn out well.

While affairs were at this triumphant juncture, Mr Freely one morning observed that a stone-carver who had been breakfasting in the eating-room had left a newspaper behind. It was the 'X——shire Gazette,' and X——shire being a county not unknown to Mr Freely, he felt some curiosity to glance over it, and especially over the advertisements. A slight flush came over his face as he read. It was produced by the following announcement: – 'If David Faux, son of Jonathan Faux, late of Gilsbrook, will apply at the office of Mr Strutt, attorney, of Rodham, he will hear of something to his advantage.'

'Father's dead!' exclaimed Mr Freely, involuntarily. 'Can he have left me a legacy?'

CHAPTER 3

Perhaps it was a result quite different from your expectations, that Mr David Faux should have returned from the West Indies only a few years after his arrival there, and have set up in his old business, like any plain man who had never travelled. But these cases do occur in life. Since, as we know, men change their skies and see new constellations without changing their souls, it will follow sometimes that they don't change their business under those novel circumstances.

Certainly, this result was contrary to David's own expectations. He had looked forward, you are aware, to a brilliant career among 'the blacks;' but, either because they had already seen too many white men, or for some other reason, they did not at once recognise him as a superior order of human being; besides, there were no princesses among them. Nobody in Jamaica was anxious to maintain David for the mere pleasure of his society; and those hidden merits of a man which are so well known to himself were as little recognised there as they notoriously are in the effete society of the Old World. So that in the dark hints that David threw out at the Oyster Club about that life of Sultanic self-indulgence spent by him in the luxurious Indies, I really think he was doing himself a wrong; I believe he worked for his bread, and, in fact, took to cooking again, as, after all, the only department in which he could offer skilled labour. He had formed several ingenious plans by which he meant to circumvent people of large fortune and small faculty; but then he never met with exactly the right people under exactly the right circumstances. David's devices for getting rich without work had apparently no direct relation with the world outside him, as his confectionery receipts had. It is possible to pass a great many bad halfpennies and bad halfcrowns, but I believe there has no instance been known of passing a halfpenny or a halfcrown as a sovereign. A sharper can drive a brisk trade in this world: it is undeniable that there may be a fine career for him, if he will dare consequences; but David was too timid to be a sharper, or venture in any way among the man-traps of the law. He dared rob nobody but his mother. And so he had to fall back on the genuine value there was in him – to be content to pass as a good halfpenny, or, to speak more accurately, as a good confectioner. For in spite of some additional reading and observation, there was nothing else he could make so much money by; nay, he found in himself even a capability of extending his skill in this direction, and embracing all forms of cookery; while, in other branches of human labour, he began to see that it was not possible for him to shine. Fate was too strong for him; he had thought to master her inclination and had fled over the seas to that end; but she caught him, tied an apron round him, and snatching him from all other devices, made him devise cakes and patties in a kitchen at Kingstown. He was getting submissive to her, since she paid him with tolerable gains; but fevers and prickly heat, and other evils incidental to cooks in ardent climates, made him long for his native land; so he took ship once more, carrying his six years' savings, and seeing distinctly, this time, what were Fate's intentions as to his career. If you question me closely as to whether all the money with which he set up at Grimworth consisted of pure and simple earnings, I am obliged to confess that he got a sum or two for charitably abstaining from mentioning 'some other people's misdemeanours. Altogether, since no prospects were attached to his family name, and since a new christening seemed a suitable commencement of a new life, Mr David Faux thought it as well to call himself Mr Edward Freely.

But lo! now, in opposition to all calculable probability, some benefit appeared to be attached to the name of David Faux. Should he neglect it, as beneath the attention of a prosperous tradesman? It might bring him into contact with his family again, and he felt no yearnings in that direction: moreover, he had small belief that the 'something to his advantage' could be anything considerable. On the other hand, even a small gain is pleasant, and the promise of it in this instance was so surprising, that David felt his curiosity awakened. The scale dipped at last on the side of writing to the lawyer, and, to be brief, the correspondence ended in an appointment for a meeting between David and his eldest brother at Mr Strutt's, the vague 'something' having been defined as a legacy from his father of eighty-two pounds three shillings.

David, you know, had expected to be disinherited; and so he would have been, if he had not, like some other indifferent sons, come of excellent parents, whose conscience made them scrupulous where much more highly-instructed people often feel themselves warranted in following the bent of their indignation. Good Mrs Faux could never forget that she had brought this ill-conditioned son into the world when he was in that entirely helpless state which excluded the smallest choice on his part; and, somehow or other, she felt that his going wrong would be his father's and mother's fault, if they failed in one tittle of their parental duty. Her notion of parental duty was not of a high and subtle kind, but it included giving him his due share of the family property; for when a man had got a little honest money of his own, was he so likely to steal? To cut the delinquent son off with a shilling, was like delivering him over to his evil propensities. No; let the sum of twenty guineas which he had stolen be deducted from his share, and then let the sum of three guineas be put back from it, seeing that his mother had always considered three of the twenty guineas as his; and, though he had run away, and was, perhaps, gone across the sea, let the money be left to him all the same, and be kept in reserve for his possible return. Mr Faux agreed to his wife's views, and made a codicil to his will accordingly, in time to die with a clear conscience. But for some time his family thought it likely that David would never reappear; and the eldest son, who had the charge of Jacob on his hands, often thought it a little hard that David might perhaps be dead, and yet, for want of certitude on that point, his legacy could not fall to his legal heir. But in this state of things the opposite certitude – namely, that David was still alive and in England – seemed to be brought by the testimony of a neighbour, who, having been on a journey to Cattelton, was pretty sure he had seen David in a gig, with a stout man driving by his side. He could 'swear it was David,' though he could 'give no account why, for he had no marks on him; but no more had a

white dog, and that didn't hinder folks from knowing a
white dog.' It was this incident which had led to the
advertisement.

The legacy was paid, of course, after a few preliminary
disclosures as to Mr David's actual position. He begged
to send his love to his mother, and to say that he hoped to
pay her a dutiful visit by-and-by; but, at present, his
business and near prospect of marriage made it difficult
for him to leave home. His brother replied with much
frankness.

'My mother may do as she likes about having you to
see her, but, for my part, I don't want to catch sight of
you on the premises again. When folks have taken a new
name, they'd better keep to their new 'quinetance.'

David pocketed the insult along with the eighty-two
pounds three, and travelled home again in some triumph
at the ease of a transaction which had enriched him to
this extent. He had no intention of offending his brother
by further claims on his fraternal recognition, and
relapsed with full contentment into the character of Mr
Edward Freely, the orphan, scion of a great but reduced
family, with an eccentric uncle in the West Indies. (I have
already hinted that he had some acquaintance with
imaginative literature; and being of a practical turn, he
had, you perceive, applied even this form of knowledge
to practical purposes.)

It was little more than a week after the return from his
fruitful journey, that the day of his marriage with Penny
having been fixed, it was agreed that Mrs Palfrey should
overcome her reluctance to move from home, and that
she and her husband should bring their two daughters to
inspect little Penny's future abode and decide on the
new arrangements to be made for the reception of the

bride. Mr Freely meant her to have a house so pretty and
comfortable that she need not envy even a wool-factor's
wife. Of course, the upper room over the shop was to be
the best sitting-room; but also the parlour behind the
shop was to be made a suitable bower for the lovely
Penny, who would naturally wish to be near her husband, though Mr Freely declared his resolution never to
allow *his* wife to wait in the shop. The decisions about the
parlour furniture were left till last, because the party was
to take tea there; and, above five o'clock, they were all
seated there with the best muffins and buttered buns
before them, little Penny blushing and smiling, with her
'crop' in the best order, and a blue frock showing her
little white shoulders, while her opinion was being
always asked and never given. She secretly wished to have
a particular sort of chimney ornaments, but she could not
have brought herself to mention it. Seated by the side of
her yellow and rather withered lover, who, though he
had not reached his thirtieth year, had already crow's-
feet about his eyes, she was quite tremulous at the
greatness of her lot in being married to a man who had
travelled so much – and before her sister Letty! The
handsome Letitia looked rather proud and contemptuous, thought her future brother-in-law an odious person, and was vexed with her father and mother for letting
Penny marry him. Dear little Penny! She certainly did
look like a fresh white-heart cherry going to be bitten off
the stem by that lipless mouth. Would no deliverer come
to make a slip between that cherry and that mouth without a lip?

'Quite a family likeness between the admiral and you,
Mr Freely,' observed Mrs Palfrey, who was looking at the
family portrait for the first time. 'It's wonderful! and

only a grand-uncle. Do you feature the rest of your family, as you know of?'

'I can't say,' said Mr Freely, with a sigh. 'My family have mostly thought themselves too high to take any notice of me.'

At this moment an extraordinary disturbance was heard in the shop, as of a heavy animal stamping about and making angry noises, and then of a glass vessel falling in shivers, while the voice of the apprentice was heard calling 'Master' in great alarm.

Mr Freely rose in anxious astonishment, and hastened into the shop, followed by the four Palfreys, who made a group at the parlour-door, transfixed with wonder at seeing a large man in a smock-frock, with a pitchfork in his hand, rush up to Mr Freely and hug him, crying out, – 'Zavy, Zavy, b'other Zavy!'

It was Jacob, and for some moments David lost all presence of mind. He felt arrested for having stolen his mother's guineas. He turned cold, and trembled in his brother's grasp.

'Why, how's this?' said Mr Palfrey, advancing from the door. 'Who is he?'

Jacob supplied the answer by saying over and over again, –

'I'se Zacob, b'other Zacob. Come 'o zee Zavy' – till hunger prompted him to relax his grasp, and to seize a large raised pie, which he lifted to his mouth.

By this time David's power of device had begun to return, but it was a very hard task for his prudence to master his rage and hatred towards poor Jacob.

'I don't know who he is; he must be drunk,' he said, in a low tone to Mr Palfrey. 'But he's dangerous with that pitchfork. He'll never let it go.' Then checking himself

on the point of betraying too great an intimacy with
Jacob's habits, he added, '*You* watch him, while I run
for the constable.' And he hurried out of the shop.

'Why, where do you come from, my man?' said Mr
Palfrey, speaking to Jacob in a conciliatory tone. Jacob
was eating his pie by large mouthfuls, and looking round
at the other good things in the shop, while he embraced
his pitchfork with his left arm and laid his left hand on
some Bath buns. He was in the rare position of a person
who recovers a long absent friend and finds him richer
than ever in the characteristics that won his heart.

'I's Zacob – b'other Zacob –'t home. I love Zavy –
b'other Zavy,' he said, as soon as Mr Palfrey had drawn
his attention. 'Zavy come back from z'Indies – got
mother's zinnies. Where's Zavy?' he added, looking
round and then turning to the others with a questioning
air, puzzled by David's disappearance.

'It's very odd,' observed Mr Palfrey to his wife and
daughters. 'He seems to say Freely's his brother come
back from th' Indies.'

'What a pleasant relation for us!' said Letitia, sarcas-
tically. 'I think he's a good deal like Mr Freely. He's got
just the same sort of nose, and his eyes are the same
colour.'

Poor Penny was ready to cry.

But now Mr Freely re-entered the shop without the
constable. During his walk of a few yards he had had
time and calmness enough to widen his view of consequences, and he saw that to get Jacob taken to the workhouse or to the lock-up house as an offensive stranger,
might have awkward effects if his family took the trouble
of inquiring after him. He must resign himself to more
patient measures.

'On second thoughts,' he said, beckoning to Mr Palfrey and whispering to him while Jacob's back was turned, 'he's a poor half-witted fellow. Perhaps his friends will come after him. I don't mind giving him something to eat, and letting him lie down for the night. He's got it into his head that he knows me – they do get these fancies, idiots do. He'll perhaps go away again in an hour or two, and make no more ado. I'm a kind-hearted man *myself* – I shouldn't like to have the poor fellow ill-used.'

'Why, he'll eat a sovereign's worth in no time,' said Mr Palfrey, thinking Mr Freely a little too magnificent in his generosity.

'Eh, Zavy, come back?' exclaimed Jacob, giving his dear brother another hug, which crushed Mr Freely's features inconveniently against the stale of the pitchfork.

'Ay, ay,' said Mr Freely, smiling, with every capability of murder in his mind, except the courage to commit it. He wished the Bath buns might by chance have arsenic in them.

'Mother's zinnies?' said Jacob, pointing to a glass jar of yellow lozenges that stood in the window. 'Zive 'em me.'

David dared not do otherwise than reach down the glass jar and give Jacob a handful. He received them in his smock-frock, which he held out for more.

'They'll keep him quiet a bit, at any rate,' thought David, and emptied the jar. Jacob grinned and mowed with delight.

'You're very good to this stranger, Mr Freely,' said Letitia; and then spitefully, as David joined the party at the parlour-door, 'I think you could hardly treat him better, if he was really your brother.'

'I've always thought it a duty to be good to idiots,' said Mr Freely, striving after the most moral view of the subject. 'We might have been idiots ourselves – everybody might have been born idiots, instead of having their right senses.'

'I don't know where there'd ha' been victual for us all then,' observed Mrs Palfrey, regarding the matter in a housewifely light.

'But let us sit down again and finish our tea,' said Mr Freely. 'Let us leave the poor creature to himself.'

They walked into the parlour again; but Jacob, not apparently appreciating the kindness of leaving him to himself, immediately followed his brother, and seated himself, pitchfork grounded, at the table.

'Well,' said Miss Letitia, rising, 'I don't know whether *you* mean to stay, mother; but I shall go home.'

'Oh, me too,' said Penny, frightened to death at Jacob, who had begun to nod and grin at her.

'Well, I think we *had* better be going, Mr Palfrey,' said the mother, rising more slowly.

Mr Freely, whose complexion had become decidedly yellower during the last half-hour, did not resist this proposition. He hoped they should meet again 'under happier circumstances.'

'It's my belief the man is his brother,' said Letitia, when they were all on their way home.

'Letty, it's very ill-natured of you,' said Penny, beginning to cry.

'Nonsense!' said Mr Palfrey. 'Freely's got no brother – he's said so many and many a time; he's an orphan; he's got nothing but uncles – leastwise, one. What's it matter what an idiot says? What call had Freely to tell lies?'

Letitia tossed her head and was silent.

Mr Freely, left alone with his affectionate brother Jacob, brooded over the possibility of luring him out of the town early the next morning, and getting him conveyed to Gilsbrook without further betrayals. But the thing was difficult. He saw clearly that if he took Jacob away himself, his absence, conjoined with the disappearance of the stranger, would either cause the conviction that he was really a relative, or would oblige him to the dangerous course of inventing a story to account for his disappearance, and his own absence at the same time. David groaned. There come occasions when falsehood is felt to be inconvenient. It would, perhaps, have been a longer-headed device, if he had never told any of those clever fibs about his uncles, grand and otherwise; for the Palfreys were simple people, and shared the popular prejudice against lying. Even if he could get Jacob away this time, what security was there that he would not come again, having once found the way? O guineas! O lozenges! what enviable people those were who had never robbed their mothers, and had never told fibs! David spent a sleepless night, while Jacob was snoring close by. Was this the upshot of travelling to the Indies, and acquiring experience combined with anecdote?

He rose at break of day, as he had once before done when he was in fear of Jacob, and took all gentle means to rouse this fatal brother from his deep sleep; he dared not be loud, because his apprentice was in the house, and would report everything. But Jacob was not to be roused. He fought out with his fist at the unknown cause of disturbance, turned over, and snored again. He must be left to wake as he would. David, with a cold perspiration on his brow, confessed to himself that Jacob could not be got away that day.

Mr Palfrey came over to Grimworth before noon, with a natural curiosity to see how his future son-in-law got on with the stranger to whom he was so benevolently inclined. He found a crowd round the shop. All Grimworth by this time had heard how Freely had been fastened on by an idiot, who called him 'Brother Zavy;' and the younger population seemed to find the singular stranger an unwearying source of fascination, while the householders dropped in one by one to inquire into the incident.

'Why don't you send him to the workhouse?' said Mr Prettyman. 'You'll have a row with him and the children presently, and he'll eat you up. The workhouse is the proper place for him; let his kin claim him, if he's got any.'

'Those may be *your* feelings, Mr Prettyman,' said David, his mind quite enfeebled by the torture of his position.

'What! *is* he your brother, then?' said Mr Prettyman, looking at his neighbour Freely rather sharply.

'All men are our brothers, and idiots particular so,' said Mr Freely, who, like many other travelled men, was not master of the English language.

'Come, come, if he's your brother, tell the truth, man,' said Mr Prettyman, with growing suspicion. 'Don't be ashamed of your own flesh and blood.'

Mr Palfrey was present, and also had his eye on Freely. It is difficult for a man to believe in the advantage of a truth which will disclose him to have been a liar. In this critical moment, David shrank from this immediate disgrace in the eyes of his future father-in-law.

'Mr Prettyman,' he said, 'I take your observations as an insult. I've no reason to be otherwise than proud of my own flesh and blood. If this poor man was my brother more than all men are, I should say so.'

A tall figure darkened the door, and David, lifting his eyes in that direction, saw his eldest brother, Jonathan, on the door-sill.

'I'll stay wi' Zavy,' shouted Jacob, as he, too, caught sight of his eldest brother; and, running behind the counter, he clutched David hard.

'What, he *is* here?' said Jonathan Faux, coming forward. 'My mother would have no nay, as he'd been away so long, but I must see after him. And it struck me he was very like come after you, because we'd been talking of you o'late, and where you lived.'

David saw there was no escape; he smiled a ghastly smile.

'What! is this a relation of yours, sir?' said Mr Palfrey to Jonathan.

'Ay, it's my innicent of a brother, sure enough,' said honest Jonathan. 'A fine trouble and cost he is to us, in th' eating and other things, but we must bear what's laid on us.'

'And your name's Freely, is it?' said Mr Prettyman.

'Nay, nay, my name's Faux, I know nothing o' Freelys,' said Jonathan, curtly. 'Come,' he added, turning to David, 'I must take some news to mother about Jacob. Shall I take him with me, or will you undertake to send him back?'

'Take him, if you can make him loose his hold of me,' said David, feebly.

'Is this gentleman here in the confectionery line your brother, then, sir?' said Mr Prettyman, feeling that it was an occasion on which formal language must be used.

'*I* don't want to own him,' said Jonathan, unable to resist a movement of indignation that had never been allowed to satisfy itself. 'He run away from home with good reasons in his pocket years ago: he didn't want to be owned again, I reckon.'

Mr Palfrey left the shop; he felt his own pride too severely wounded by the sense that he had let himself be fooled, to feel curiosity for further details. The most pressing business was to go home and tell his daughter that Freely was a poor sneak, probably a rascal, and that her engagement was broken off.

Mr Prettyman stayed, with some internal self-gratulation that *he* had never given in to Freely, and that Mr Chaloner would see now what sort of fellow it was that he had put over the heads of older parishioners. He considered it due from him (Mr Prettyman) that, for the interests of the parish, he should know all that was to be known about this 'interloper.' Grimworth would have people coming from Botany Bay to settle in it, if things went on in this way.

It soon appeared that Jacob could not be made to quit his dear brother David except by force. He understood, with a clearness equal to that of the most intelligent mind, that Jonathan would take him back to skimmed milk, apple-dumpling, broad-beans, and pork. And he had found a paradise in his brother's shop. It was a difficult matter to use force with Jacob, for he wore heavy nailed boots; and if his pitchfork had been mastered, he would have resorted without hesitation to kicks. Nothing short of using guile to bind him hand and foot would have made all parties safe.

'Let him stay,' said David, with desperate resignation,

frightened above all things at the idea of further distur-
bances in his shop, which would make his exposure all
the more conspicuous. '*You* go away again, and to-
morrow I can, perhaps, get him to go to Gilsbrook with
me. He'll follow me fast enough, I daresay,' he added,
with a half-groan.

'Very well,' said Jonathan, gruffly. 'I don't see why
you shouldn't have some trouble and expense with him
as well as the rest of us. But mind you bring him back safe
and soon, else mother 'll never rest.'

On this arrangement being concluded, Mr Prettyman
begged Mr Jonathan Faux to go and take a snack with
him, an invitation which was quite acceptable; and as
honest Jonathan had nothing to be ashamed of, it is
probable that he was very frank in his communications to
the civil draper, who, pursuing the benefit of the parish,
hastened to make all the information he could gather
about Freely common parochial property. You may
imagine that the meeting of the Club at the Woolpack
that evening was unusually lively. Every member was
anxious to prove that he had never liked Freely, as he
called himself. Faux was his name, was it? Fox would
have been more suitable. The majority expressed a desire
to see him hooted out of the town.

Mr Freely did not venture over his door-sill that day,
for he knew Jacob would keep at his side, and there was
every probability that they would have a train of juvenile
followers. He sent to engage the Woolpack gig for an
early hour the next morning; but this order was not kept
religiously a secret by the landlord. Mr Freely was
informed that he could not have the gig till seven; and
the Grimworth people were early risers. Perhaps they
were more alert than usual on this particular morning; for

when Jacob, with a bag of sweets in his hand, was induced to mount the gig with his brother David, the inhabitants of the market-place were looking out of their doors and windows, and at the turning of the street there was even a muster of apprentices and schoolboys, who shouted as they passed in what Jacob took to be a very merry and friendly way, nodding and grinning in return. 'Huzzay, David Faux! how's your uncle?' was their morning's greeting. Like other pointed things, it was not altogether impromptu.

Even this public derision was not so crushing to David as the horrible thought that though he might succeed now in getting Jacob home again there would never be any security against his coming back, like a wasp to the honey-pot. As long as David lived at Grimworth, Jacob's return would be hanging over him. But could he go on living at Grimworth – an object of ridicule, discarded by the Palfreys, after having revelled in the consciousness that he was an envied and prosperous confectioner? David liked to be envied; he minded less about being loved.

His doubts on this point were soon settled. The mind of Grimworth became obstinately set against him and his viands, and the new school being finished, the eating-room was closed. If there had been no other reason, sympathy with the Palfreys, that respectable family who had lived in the parish time out of mind, would have determined all well-to-do people to decline Freely's goods. Besides, he had absconded with his mother's guineas: who knew what else he had done, in Jamaica or elsewhere, before he came to Grimworth, worming himself into families under false pretences? Females shuddered. Dreadful suspicions gathered round him: his green eyes, his bow-legs, had a criminal aspect. The rector disliked the sight of a man who had imposed upon him; and all boys who could not afford to purchase, hooted 'David Faux' as they passed his shop. Certainly no man now would pay anything for the 'goodwill' of Mr Freely's business, and he would be obliged to quit it without a peculium so desirable towards defraying the expense of moving.

In a few months the shop in the market-place was again to let, and Mr David Faux, *alias* Mr Edward Freely, had gone – nobody at Grimworth knew whither. In this way the demoralisation of Grimworth women was checked. Young Mrs Steene renewed her efforts to make light mince-pies, and having at last made a batch so excellent that Mr Steene looked at her with complacency as he ate them, and said they were the best he had ever eaten in his life, she thought less of bulbuls and renegades ever after. The secrets of the finer cookery were revived in the breasts of matronly housewives, and daughters were again anxious to be initiated in them.

You will further, I hope, be glad to hear, that some purchases of drapery made by pretty Penny, in preparation for her marriage with Mr Freely, came in quite as well for her wedding with young Towers as if they had been made expressly for the latter occasion. For Penny's complexion had not altered, and blue always became it best.

Here ends the story of Mr David Faux, confectioner, and his brother Jacob. And we see in it, I think, an admirable instance of the unexpected forms in which the great Nemesis hides herself.

45, Pall Mall, S.W.
May 3 1864

My dear Madam

It was only yesterday afternoon that I clearly understood from Mr Lewes that I was to regard 'Brother Jacob' as a present from you – I can hardly tell you how much I was touched and gratified by your kindness. The gift is a princely one in value, and it comes to me at a time when it is even more than ordinarily valuable; but you will I am sure understand me, when I say that it is not chiefly on that account that I am pleased at receiving such a present from you. I hope that I may regard it as an indication of your satisfaction with the manner in which our business relations have been conducted as well as of your feeling of personal kindness towards myself, and I value your good opinion so highly that such an expression of it is deeply gratifying to me. I cannot sufficiently thank you for it.

Wishing you and Mr Lewes perfect enjoyment of your trip

I remain
My dear Madam
Your very faithful & obliged
Mrs Lewes   G Smith

This hitherto unpublished letter to George Eliot that from the first publisher of *Brother Jacob*, George Smith, is reproduced by kind permission of The Beinecke Rare Book and Manuscript Library, Yale University.

AFTERWORD

Among George Eliot's works of fiction, only one has been more neglected than *The Lifted Veil*, and that is her only other short story, *Brother Jacob*. Neither Gillian Beer nor Jennifer Uglow in their recent full-length appraisals of the author's achievement refer to it at all, though both discuss *The Lifted Veil* – Jennifer Uglow quite extensively.[1] When the story isn't entirely overlooked, it is usually almost parenthetically denigrated as 'rather cheerless and austere' (U.C. Knoepflmacher)[2] or cynical and coldly sarcastic (Gordon S. Haight).[3] W.J. Harvey is even more contemptuous. In *The Art of George Eliot*, he refers to it just once, and then only to dismiss it as 'that tedious tale'.[4]

Why, then, reissue it? One obvious reason is that modern readers of George Eliot cannot assess the story for themselves unless it is made more readily available to them – and it has not been published since 1906.[5] It was not, after all, discarded by its author. Written in August 1860 – that is, a few months after *The Mill on the Floss* was finished, and just before *Silas Marner* was embarked upon – it is true that George Eliot claimed to regard it as a 'trifle',[6] but she wanted it published and cared about its presentation. The other – and more compelling – reason for reissuing it is that it deserves much better

59

treatment than the twentieth century has so far accorded
it. It is time that it was spoken up for.

Not that 'Brother Jacob' has always been unappre-
ciated. François D'Albert-Durade – in whose house in
Geneva George Eliot had lived from October 1849 to
March 1850, and who remained a lifelong friend – liked
it enough to go to the trouble of translating it[7] (though,
true to more recent form, Gordon Haight, the editor of
George Eliot's letters, omits it from his list of D'Albert-
Durade's translations of her fiction);[8] and Henry James
reviewed it favourably for the *Nation* when, in accor-
dance with George Eliot's own wish, it appeared (1878)
with *Silas Marner* and *The Lifted Veil* in the Cabinet
edition of her works. It is true that James thought it 'a
little injured, perhaps, by an air of effort'; by the
conscious attempts to be epigrammatic and pregnantly
witty.

> But the figure of the diminutively mean and sneaking
> young man upon whom the great Nemesis descends is a real
> portrait; it is an admirable picture of unromantic mal-
> feasance. Capital, too, is the fatal Jacob, who, after the
> manner of idiots, leaves us with a sense of his combined
> vagueness and obstructiveness. The minor touches are very
> brilliant, and the story is, generally, excellent reading.[9]

It was James' opinion that those who turn to this story
and to its single companion, *The Lifted Veil* (which he
thought rather less successful), 'will doubtless wonder
why the author has not oftener attempted to express
herself within the limits of that form of fiction which the
French call the *nouvelle*.'[10] So far this hasn't proved to be
the case. Greatly admired though George Eliot's
'spacious' (James' word again) novels are, her latter-day

critics are more inclined to wonder why she expressed herself at all in the more constraining form.

This is a pity, for despite their flaws (the handling of the revivification scene in *The Lifted Veil* and the occasional epigrammatic intrusiveness noted by James in *Brother Jacob*), these stories – which are quite unlike each other – are in fact very adroit. When we add them to George Eliot's first fiction, *Scenes of Clerical Life* – which, though bonded together, are independent entities – we can see that the challenge of the disciplines imposed by the *nouvelle* was not necessarily at odds with her impulse also to write expansively. *Silas Marner* – following hot on the heels of *Brother Jacob*, and arguably her most nearly perfect work – testifies to this, for it is hardly spacious in the Jamesian sense. In fact, it turns out (somewhat surprisingly) to be slightly shorter than 'Janet's Repentance', the last of the *Scenes*. In between that story and *Silas Marner*, and apart from *Silas'* two fellows in the Cabinet edition, George Eliot of course produced *Adam Bede* and *The Mill on the Floss*; so her departure from the short story model was not a steady process charting her development (as James claimed it to be), but a breaking-off. Consequently, in exchange for a sympathetic balance between the epic possibilities of the novel and the narrative succinctness of the tales, a sometimes oppressive conflict developed between grandiose schemes for poems and her genius for prose.

The reason George Eliot failed to write any more short stories after *Brother Jacob* was not, I think, that she lost interest in the *genre*, but simply that she had not received the necessary encouragement. Although George Smith, who was to publish *Romola*, offered George Eliot two hundred and fifty guineas for the story in February

1862, it had already been rejected by *Harper*'s agent, Sampson Low. Smith wanted the story for his *Cornhill* magazine, but because it was too short to divide into the three numbers immediately required, it didn't appear until July 1864, when George Eliot made a gratefully received present of it to compensate the publisher for the financial failure of *Romola*. It was published anonymously, just as *The Lifted Veil* had been – John Blackwood's decision – when it first appeared in *Blackwood's Magazine*. Then, in 1866, Blackwood excluded both stories from the new Cheap Edition of the 'recognised' series of George Eliot's works. No public acknowledgement was countenanced until the appearance in 1878 of the comprehensive Cabinet edition, which elicited James' comments. It isn't surprising, therefore, that the always diffident author – haunted, as Lewes said, by 'the idea of her own failure'[11] – proffered no further specimens of this type. Had James been the stories' first objective critic instead of Blackwood or Low, the case might have been different.

Brother Jacob is not, nor does it aspire to be, a great work (though it is certainly highly individual), and its protagonist, David Faux, is probably George Eliot's most unpleasant character, as Knoepflmacher suggests.[12] What is remarkable is that, since James, even her most searching and sympathetic critics have failed to recognise – let alone enjoy – the exuberance with which she created such unpleasantness.

The joy of David is his mental activity. Like his crime (the theft of his doting mother's hoard of twenty guineas), David's mind is small and squalid, but it seethes with self-aggrandising fantasies and furtive inventiveness. It is a mark of George Eliot's own inventiveness that she allows herself to inhabit such a mind in order to pursue its gratifications and bowl it swiftly towards its nemesis. But her method of presenting David's portrait is quite different from that she had employed for Maggie Tulliver, his immediate predecessor. Maggie's personality and morality are subtle and complex. Her development is analysed, and each stage in her growth is psychologically accounted for. David, on the other hand, is a fabular hero. He therefore is not only morally complete at the beginning of his story, but must wear his moral nature in his physical aspects; and George Eliot depicts his unprepossessing image with great relish. Instead of producing a set description of the total man, she doles out his attributes, allowing them to assemble as the tale proceeds. Each attribute seems more unappealing than the last, or is made increasingly unappealing through constant repetition. Each one corroborates every other, as 'timid green eyes', for example, are added to a physiognomy already noted as 'pasty' and 'lipless'. Topped by 'stumpy hair', this visage becomes variously 'sallow', 'pale', 'pallid', 'peaky', and 'yellow' when David – now calling himself Mr Edward Freely – surfaces in Grimworth after nearly six years in Jamaica to work his way stealthily upwards towards a prestigious engagement and a delectable fiancée. Offset on one side by the guileless Penny's pink-and-white roundness and flaxen ringlets, and on the other by the ardent blushes and dark whiskers of Penny's suitor, the wholesome young Towers, the disadvantages of David's by this time prematurely withered complexion are further enhanced by 'crow's-feet about the eyes'. Thus completed, the portrait is mounted upon a pair of bow legs.

The point about David Faux is not that he is wicked,

but that he is sordid. Because everything about his ambitions, his actions, and his sentiments is trivial and mean, he lacks the glamour of a fully-fledged villain. However, although he is no red-blooded Falstaff, but a piece of disgusting vermin fit only for the attentions of Mr Towers' valuable ferret, he is no less than Falstaff a figure of vice. For him, of course, there is no quasi-heroic rejection of honour; no expansiveness; no excess – since for the confectionery to which he 'irrevocably' weds himself his appetite soon sickens. He makes no lovable gestures that condemn others to perish. He represents a commoner cry of wretches whose currish acts deprive others merely of life's consolations. Where Falstaff is great, David is meagre.

This moral dinginess is undoubtedly depressing, yet the story itself is not because David is so satisfactorily punished. In fact, the whole mode of *Brother Jacob* is George Eliot's antidote to the effect on her of producing the last volume of *The Mill on the Floss*, which she had written 'in a drive of feeling'[13] crying herself 'almost into stupor, over visions of sorrow'.[14] No matter how slight we may consider the story to be, the fact that it was the next work to emerge after *The Mill* is of consequence, for the rhythms of George Eliot's creative life are very revealing.

I have suggested elsewhere that, before she could commit Maggie Tulliver to her great renunciation, she needed first to create Maggie's moral alternative: Latimer, the hero of *The Lifted Veil*.[15] It is as though she couldn't condemn her loved heroine to her self-sacrificial isolation until she had established a worse fate, the isolation and inner barrenness that results from Latimer's reckless pursuit of self-gratification. George Eliot's treatment of her clairvoyant hero is sombre because the pro-

foundly serious moral concerns of his story are a preparation for the novel that was to follow. The theme of
Brother Jacob is also serious, but, as James recognised,
the treatment of the theme turns it into a sort of game, of
which the rules must have been psychologically very
refreshing for George Eliot to follow. Contemplating as
she was a commitment to the 'Italian story' that was to
become *Romola*, she had first to complete her disen-
gagement from *The Mill*. Grimworth society and the
brothers Faux would have helped to distance that great
novel and its emotional ravages by dealing more play-
fully with the implacable forces – narrowness, mean-
spiritedness, petty righteousness – against which Maggie
had struggled.

If *Brother Jacob* helped George Eliot to let go of the
heroine to whom she was so bound, it also, I think, helps
to account for the fact that *Silas Marner* 'thrust itself'[16]
between her and the prospect of *Romola*; for, just as the
little 'fable' was a by-product of the novel before it, so,
in essence, was it a precursor of the next.

The links of a creative chain are not randomly assem-
bled, as George Eliot was aware. 'I like my writings to
appear in the order in which they are written,' she said,
'because they belong to successive mental phases'.[17] By
choosing to omit, as we invariably have done, *Brother
Jacob* from the chain, we have allowed ourselves to regard
the tale as an anomaly. But we should be grateful for its
existence not only for its own sake, but because the ideas
that it embodies also engendered *Silas Marner*. It is true
that story and novel pursue their shared ideas to different – even opposite – ends, but the negative and murky
ethos represented in the character of David Faux stands
in the same relation to Silas' luminous redemption as

Latimer's values and fate stand in relation to Maggie's. Each of the larger works has a debt to, and maintains its connection with, the lesser work that immediately preceded it.

The judgement expressed in the last sentence of the story of David and his pitchfork-waving, moral incubus of an idiot brother, Jacob (whose awful robustness George Eliot also uncompromisingly enjoyed), applies equally – though less obviously or directly – to the weaver's story: 'And we see in it, I think, an admirable instance of the unexpected forms in which the great Nemesis hides herself.' This concluding reference in *Brother Jacob* to 'the great Nemesis' points directly to one of the central concerns of *Silas Marner*. After receiving approximately two thirds of this novel, John Blackwood expressed the view that it needed 'brighter lights and some characters of whom one can think with pleasure as fellow creatures'.[18] George Eliot replied that, in fact, *Silas* 'sets – or is intended to set – in a strong light the remedial influences of pure, natural human relations. The Nemesis is a very mild one.'[19] It is true that the form in which Nemesis hides herself in *Silas Marner* is different from the form she had taken in *Brother Jacob*. For one thing, in the novel her eye is not on the main protagonist, but on Godfrey Cass, who is to be punished for his deception of Nancy, and for failing to acknowledge his motherless infant daughter, by that daughter's filial rejection of him when he makes his belated claim. The retribution is 'mild' because Godfrey is allowed to 'mend a bit'[20] and to keep his loyal wife. In *Brother Jacob*, Nemesis gleefully exposes Mr Freely ('Faux was his name, was it? Fox would have been more suitable') before obliging him to slink off 'without a peculium so desirable towards defraying the expense of moving'.[21] Nevertheless, since it is on retributive justice that Silas' happiness depends, it is Nemesis who controls the mechanism of both stories.

In each case, the mechanism is attached to a symbolically gleaming hoard of coins. Silas' honestly-accumulated treasure is of course replaced by Eppie's golden curls (though it ultimately returns); while, increased by dubious means, David's stolen guineas transmogrify into the ultimately forfeited prize of Miss Penny Palfrey's 'yellowish flaxen hair', which is teased into 'bright crisp' artificial ringlets that form 'smooth, perfect miniature tubes'. In other words, Miss Penny (a good-natured Hetty Sorrel) is Eppie's ironic counterpart, just as David Faux – a self-exiled thief – is the ironic counterpart to Silas, a thief's exiled victim. And there are other links. As immigrants, both David and Silas are subjected to the superstitious judgements of their neighbours, and in each case the outsider's eyes inspire the judgements. But where Silas' strange unearthly gaze is suggestive of evil only until the theft of his hoard establishes his human vulnerability and human-kindness, the windows of David's soul fail to reveal the criminal within before his ignominious past comes to light.

In *Brother Jacob*, the suggestive multiplication of 'magic' numbers (as the youngest of seven brothers, David had been promised three of his mother's twenty guineas – or twenty-one sovereigns) modifies the allegoric mode, which is itself sustained by devices such as the satiric use of fraternally biblical names (David, Jacob, and Jonathan), or names indicating type (Strutt, Prettyman, Palfrey, and so on). The function of the owners of these names is not strictly to personify a specific

attribute, however (though, as a whole, Grimworth society virtually amounts to a personification of provincial
complacency), but to encourage the readers' notions of a
particular genre to associate themselves with the story; so
that by the time the Grimworthians recognise Faux to be
Fox, the fabular atmosphere has established itself naturally, as it were. This technique is reversed in *Silas
Marner*, which retains an essence of the 'sort of legendary
tale' that George Eliot first conceived *despite* the 'realis-
tic treatment'[22] she chose after all to give it. It is this
legendary quality that permits a sense of the miraculous
to pervade the narrative logic.

The quotation George Eliot took for her story's motto
is the clue to its nature:

> 'Trompeurs, c'est pour vous que j'écris,
>   Attendez vous à la pareille.'
>   LA FONTAINE

But though familiarity with the context of these lines
increases our understanding of George Eliot's intentions,
it is not absolutely necessary for us to know that they
conclude the fable of 'The Fox and the Stork' in order to
appreciate the nature of the entertainment in store: the
acknowledgement to La Fontaine introduces us at once to
the appropriate realm. The fact that David is indeed the
Fox of his 'fable' points the connection, but no reader is
expected solemnly to identify himself as a 'trompeur' for
whom David's career will have specific application.[23]
George Eliot's inclination seems less to instruct than to
define a particular (yet common) strain of ill nature, and
she pursues her idea on its own terms. The reference to La
Fontaine and the subsequent fabular allusions therefore
create a suitable medium for the tale without necessarily

turning it into a generic imitation. Altogether, the pacey, economic narrative style, the social simplifications, the moral scale, and the forms in which temptation presents itself (to the youth and female population of Grimworth as well as to David) suggest that *Brother Jacob* was conceived as a sort of children's story for adults. The spirit in which it is read therefore matters greatly. If we insist on assessing its philosophical attitudes and social analyses in terms that are appropriate for *The Mill* or *Silas*, we unfairly burden it, seek what isn't there, and overlook what it is.

The terms of *Brother Jacob* are indicated by David's own literary tastes. Early in the story we are told that he had read some novels borrowed from the circulating library, and had even gone so far as to *buy* the story of 'Inkle and Yarico', 'which had made him feel very sorry for poor Mr Inkle'.

The story of which 'poor Mr Inkle' is the hero is hardly known today, but its popularity lasted throughout the eighteenth century and into the nineteenth. The original version, related by Steele in the first volume of the *Spectator*,[24] inspired many sequels – mainly poetic – by different hands and in several languages until, in 1787, it was taken up by George Colman junior and inflated into a musical play, *Inkle and Yarico*, which was mounted very successfully at both Covent Garden and the Haymarket, London. It is difficult to be quite sure which version George Eliot imagined David bought. I agree with Dale that she was probably acquainted with Colman's play, which may have given her the idea for *Brother Jacob*.[25] However, the fact that she refers informally to an unspecified 'story' suggests that she was familiar with that story, and expected her readers to be familiar with it, in the way that we are familiar with, say, the story of Dick Whittington; for, as Lawrence Marsden Price suggests, it seems to have been on the verge of passing into folklore.[26]

Whatever version David knew, the essential parallel between the Inkle and Yarico story and *Brother Jacob* is that both are variations on the time-honoured theme of fortune-seeking. Insofar as he crosses the seas in search not of adventure, but of personal gain, Inkle provides a sympathetic pattern for David; for, as George Eliot puts it with characteristic irony, 'When a man is not adequately appreciated or comfortably placed in his own country, his thoughts naturally turn towards foreign climes'. David's own thoughts turn first towards Liverpool and America, and then, like Inkle's, towards the West Indies.

The relevant factor in both Steele's and Colman's account is that it concerns a young city merchant whose ship anchors off the coast of America before proceeding to Barbados. On shore, Inkle and his companions are pursued by 'savages', but Inkle (alone in the *Spectator*, accompanied by his factotum, Trudge, in Colman) is protected by the anything but savage Yarico, who falls in love with him. There is much idyllic dalliance before Inkle is reunited with his kind and conveyed to Barbados, taking Yarico with him. Here the accounts diverge. Steele's Yarico is ruthlessly sold, despite the fact that she is 'with child', whereas, in Colman, the Governor of Barbados refuses to permit the sale. In the former, Inkle is not called to account. In the latter he is made to reform in the last scene (he really has no practical option since the bride who was to secure his advancement has organised a more desirable bridegroom for herself). Suddenly acknowledging his commitment to Yarico, Inkle clasps her to his bosom. 'All sing' – though nothing so offensive to an eighteenth-century audience as their actual wedding takes place. Nevertheless, the fact that Inkle is finally lumbered with the copper-coloured Yarico is sufficient reason for David to pity him and to fantasise that, with his own 'easily recognisable merit of whiteness', some Princess Yarico would want him to marry her, and make him presents of very large jewels beforehand; after which, he needn't marry her unless he liked.

The direct and indirect allusions to Inkle's story weld the elements of folklore to those of fable. But George Eliot's purpose in creating this amalgam is not merely to see whether she could bring off a certain kind of literary experiment (though I am very taken with Dale's idea that she and Lewes 'were engaged in a friendly competition in the art of fable writing').[27] Whatever instigated *Brother Jacob*, its medium adapted itself according to one of George Eliot's abiding concerns, which was to examine the forms in which temptation presents itself, and to consider the consequences of yielding to it. Her first premise is that the forms themselves depend on the nature of the yearnings (which in turn depend on the moral natures) of those who are to be tempted. The second is that the tempting should take place in, or promise access to, some appropriate paradise.

George Eliot had recently left Maggie Tulliver after conducting her through her desperate struggle to remain true to her own beliefs. Her identification with Maggie's suffering had been complete because there had been complete sympathy between her own sensibility and her heroine's. It was necessary for David Faux to be as different as possible from Maggie; therefore, where her spirit is

generous in all its manifestations, his is in every sense
stunted. This contrast is reflected in their childhood per-
ceptions of Paradise. Maggie's perception is permeated
by love of brother and father, and love of place. It is not
without delicious things to eat, but nuts and cake and
fruit can be savoured only when shared, and only in
association with spiritual comfort. David's perception,
on the other hand, is represented by a garish display of
'glass jars full of sugared almonds and pink lozenges'. It
is of course this sickly projection of his own greed that
lures him into the confectionery trade, whereupon it is
supplanted by the visions of 'very large jewels' and a life
relieved of the necessity to labour by subservient Black
people.[28] But though David's idea of perfect bliss is thus
broadened, he has pledged himself to sugar. It is therefore in sugar that his course is plotted, and it is by sugar
that he is ultimately trapped. In mock anticipation of the
transformation of Silas Marner's hard golden coins into
Eppie's soft golden curls, David beguiles Jacob – who
has discovered the stolen hoard – into secrecy by demon-
strating that merely clinking 'zinnies' become, when
buried, the ambrosia of sweet yellow lozenges. But the
ensuing 'life of Sultanic self-indulgence' eludes David
(though he judges Penny 'to be of submissive temper –
likely to wait upon him as well as if she had been a
negress'). Instead, Fate 'caught him, tied an apron round
him, and . . . made him devise cakes and patties in a
kitchen in Kingstown'. It is therefore as the confectioner-
pastry cook Edward Freely that David manifests himself
in Grimworth, where the first matron to give way to the
temptation of his luxurious arrangement of pies, sauces,
and bottled fruit is the veterinary surgeon's wife, whose
imagination is in any case already weakened by a diet of

literary confections by Byron and Thomas Moore. For the children, David mounts a dazzling exhibition in which

> there was predominance of the more delicate hues of pink, and white, and yellow, and buff, in the abundant lozenges, candies, sweet biscuits and icings, which to the eyes of a bilious person might easily have been blended into a faëry landscape in Turner's latest style . . . [The children] almost forgot to go to their dinner that day, their appetites being preoccupied with imaginary sugar-plums.

In this sugar-lair, the disguised fox waits for, and profits from, his prey. Inevitably, however, the lure draws the insatiably sweet-toothed idiot, who, having indeed 'found a paradise in his brother's shop', ecstatically and fatally claims him. Exposed, the Tempter is expelled from his own Garden.

One of the problems of approaching *Brother Jacob* with our expectations of George Eliot already primed is that it is her only work lacking a character with whom we can properly sympathise. David's simple, loving, scrupulous mother isn't allowed to come sufficiently into focus for us to perceive her as an individual; but neither are we meant to. In keeping with the mode of the tale, she evokes a literary tradition – especially when she becomes the *widowed* mother – without being reduced to an allegorical type. Her function is to lend tone to David's portrait, for a beloved youngest son who steals from a mother whom he proposes not to visit even in her widowhood, is of course more wretched than a young man who merely steals.

What makes the story 'excellent reading' is its skilful organisation. It is a little story about a petty, mean-spirited criminal who disrupts the tenor of narrow lives filled with small anxieties and small vanities. Exploited by David, these anxieties and vanities corrupt into petty dishonesty (herein lies the lesson), but, with David gone, 'the demoralisation of Grimworth women was checked', and no one, except David, is punished or harmed. But it is only in fiction that humanity can rid itself so neatly and deftly of such as he, which is why *Brother Jacob* does not pretend to be 'life'.

Beryl Gray, London, 1988

NOTES

1 Gillian Beer, *George Eliot*, *Key Women Writers*, Harvester, Brighton, 1986 and Jennifer Uglow, *George Eliot*, *Virago Pioneers*, Virago Press, London, 1987.

2 U.C. Knoepflmacher, *George Eliot's Early Novels*, p. 224, University of California Press, Berkeley and Los Angeles, 1968.

3 Gordon S. Haight, *George Eliot: A Biography*, p. 340, Clarendon Press, Oxford, 1968.

4 W.J. Harvey, *The Art of George Eliot*, p. 212, Chatto & Windus, London, 1961.

5 *Silas Marner, The Lifted Veil, Brother Jacob* in The Works of George Eliot, vol. III, The Worlds Classics, Henry Frowde, Oxford University Press, London, New York and Toronto. Theodore Watts-Dunton devotes his ten pages of Introduction to *Silas Marner* and *The Lifted Veil*, claiming that 'lack of space' prevents his commenting on *Brother Jacob*.

6 Gordon S. Haight (ed), *The George Eliot Letters*, vol. IV, p. 157, Yale University Press, New Haven and London, 1954–78.

7 *Letters*, vol. IV, p. 428.

8 *Letters*, vol. I. p. xiv.

9 Henry James, 'The Lifted Veil' and 'Brother Jacob', the *Nation*, 26, p. 277, 25 April 1878. Reprinted in Gordon S. Haight (ed), *A Century of George Eliot Criticism*, p. 131, *University Paperback*, Methuen, London, 1966.

10 Henry James in *A Century of George Eliot Criticism*, p. 131.

11 *Letters*, III, p. 380.

12 Knoepflmacher, p. 224.

13 *Letters*, III, p. 267.

14 *Letters*, III, p. 271.

15 My Afterword to *The Lifted Veil*, *Virago Classics*, Virago Press, London, 1985.

16 *Letters*, III, p. 360.

17 *Letters*, III, pp. 382–3.

18 *Letters*, III, p. 380.

19 *Letters*, III, p. 382.

20 *Silas Marner*, p. 264, Cabinet edition, W. M. Blackwood & Sons, Edinburgh and London, 1878.

21 Both Gordon Haight in *Letters*, vol. III, p. 380, note 7, and Peter Allan Dale in 'George Eliot's "Brother Jacob": Fables and the Physiology of Common Life', *Philological Quarterly*, 64(1), Winter, 1885, p. 29, assume that it is *Dunstan* Cass who is made to encounter Nemesis, but it is unlikely that it was the wastrel Dunstan to whom Blackwood referred when he regretted that George Eliot had 'done for the only one of the Cass family who had anything about him to redeem the breed' (*Letters*, vol. III, p. 380). Dunstan does indeed fall into the Stone-pit and drown immediately after robbing Silas, but George Eliot would hardly describe such a fate as 'mild'. Furthermore, although the discovery of his skeleton wedged near Silas' coins and Godfrey's hunting-whip (also crowned with gold) is highly dramatic, we know nothing of Dunstan's dark journey between his deed and his death. His despatch, though absolute, is summary; dramatised retroactively much later in the novel, and only in our own imaginations. This brilliant touch allows George Eliot to permit Nemesis to concentrate her subtler faculties on Godfrey, who deserves them for having placed his trust in 'some unforeseen turn of fortune, some favourable chance'; 'some throw of fortune's dice' (*Silas Marner*, Cabinet Edition, p. 112).

22 *Letters*, III, p. 382.

23 The fable describes how the fox tricked the stork out of her dinner by serving it on a plate from which only he could lap, and how the stork retaliated by inviting the fox to a dinner which she served in a vase fit only for her long beak. Translated by Robert Thomson, the last four lines read:

> Poor renard blush'd a fowl should trick him so,
> Chop-and-tail-fall'n, fasting oblig'd to go.
>
> Deceivers all I write for you,
> Measure for measure waits you too.

Robert Thomson (trans.), *La Fontaine's Fables*, vol. I, p. 30, Chenu, Paris, 1806.

24 The *Spectator*, Tuesday 13 March 1711. Steele's brief anecdote is in fact an embellishment of an account by a seventeenth-century traveller of the plight of a handsome Indian woman, Yarico, who was taken to Barbados and sold into slavery by a young merchant whose life she had saved. She was subsequently made pregnant by a white 'Christian' servant. See Richard Ligon, *A True Exact History of the Island of Barbados*, pp. 54–55, Humphrey Moseley, London, 1657. The name 'Inkle' is Steele's invention.

25 Dale, *Philological Quarterly*, p. 33, note 11. I think it is unlikely, though,

that the idea came to her 'from her research in late eighteenth-century, early nineteenth-century operas for Book 6 of *The Mill on the Floss*' (p. 20), since the music that is certainly crucial to that novel is music that George Eliot had herself absorbed. Given Lewes' fascination with and knowledge of the theatre (he was, after all, a critic, and had both written plays and acted enthusiastically in Dickens' troupe), she may have known about *Inkle and Yarico* through him. What is most likely, however, is that she came across it in Volume 16 of *Cumberland's British Theatre*, John Cumberland, London, 1829–c.1875, a work with which she and Lewes were certain to have been familiar. In his 'Remarks' prefacing this edition of the play, George Daniel acknowledges that the play is borrowed from the 'well-known tale' in the *Spectator*, which corroborates the view that the story was current independently of the play.

26 Lawrence Marsden Price, *The Inkle and Yarico Album*, p. 47, University of California Press, Berkeley, 1937. I am indebted to Dale, *Philological Quarterly*, p. 33, note 12 for drawing attention to the existence of this work.

27 Dale, *Philological Quarterly*, pp. 32–33, note 10. It is interesting that Lewes' story, 'Mrs Beauchamp's Vengeance', *Blackwood's Magazine*, 89, pp. 537–54, 1861, is also based on a fox fable: 'The Fox and the Grapes'. However, Lewes inverts the point of the original, in which the fox declares the desired grapes to be sour because they are out of reach. Lewes' tale is about what happens when the grapes (a desirable young widow) seem to hang within reach of the fox (a philandering portrait-painter, whose bluff the widow calls).

28 George Eliot's irony concerning the white and weedy David's sense of superiority over 'the blacks' is a significant comment on Colman's play, which, though superficial, is nevertheless an indicator to the prevailing late eighteenth-century racial attitudes it purports to satirise. Yarico has a Step 'n'Fetchit maid called Wowski, for example, who falls to the happy lot of Trudge. Relishing her as 'a nice little plump bit', Trudge plans to take Wowski back to London, install her in 'a couple of snug rooms on a first floor', supply her with a white boy to bring up the tea-kettle, and visit her every evening after he has finished work in his master's counting-house. It is to his credit that he refuses to sell Wowski at the 'Black Fair' at Barbados, where Patty (maid to Inkle's intended) refers variously to savages and 'Hottypots', and has no difficulty in identifying Yarico as a 'black-a-moor'.

VIRAGO MODERN CLASSICS

The first Virago Modern Classic, *Frost in May* by Antonia White, was published in 1978. It launched a list dedicated to the celebration of women writers and to the rediscovery and reprinting of their works. Its aim was, and is, to demonstrate the existence of a female tradition in fiction which is both enriching and enjoyable. The Leavisite notion of the 'Great Tradition', and the narrow, academic definition of a 'classic', has meant the neglect of a large number of interesting secondary works of fiction. In calling the series 'Modern Classics' we do not necessarily mean 'great' — although this is often the case. Published with new critical and biographical introductions, books are chosen for many reasons: sometimes for their importance in literary history; sometimes because they illuminate particular aspects of womens' lives, both personal and public. They may be classics of comedy or storytelling; their interest can be historical, feminist, political or literary.

Initially the Virago Modern Classics concentrated on English novels and short stories published in the early decades of this century. As the series has grown it has broadened to include works of fiction from different centuries, different countries, cultures and literary traditions. In 1984 the Victorian Classics were launched; there are separate lists of Irish, Scottish, European, American, Australian and other English speaking countries; there are books written by Black women, by Catholic and Jewish women, and a few relevant novels by men. There is, too, a companion series of Non-Fiction Classics constituting biography, autobiography, travel, journalism, essays, poetry, letters and diaries.

By the end of 1989 over 300 titles will have been published in these two series, many of which have been suggested by our readers.

Also of Interest

THE LIFTED VEIL
George Eliot

"I long for life, and there is no help. I thirsted for the unknown: the thirst is gone. O God, let me stay with the known, and be weary of it: I am content"

Latimer, a sensitive and intellectual man, finds he has clairvoyant powers. Then he has a vision of a woman, "pale, fatal-eyed", whom he later meets: she is Bertha Grant, his brother's fiancée. Entranced, bewildered, Latimer falls under her spell, unwilling to take heed of the warning visions which beset him. In 1859 George Eliot interrupted her work on *The Mill on the Floss* to write this unusual novella. Reminiscent of Mary Shelley and Mary E. Braddon, *The Lifted Veil* embarrassed her publishers by its exploration of the "psuedosciences" and its publication was delayed. It first appeared in 1878, together with *Silas Marner* and *Brother Jacob* in a Cabinet edition of George Eliot's work and was not published as a single volume until 1924. A chilling tale of moral alienation and despair, this forgotten novella testifies to George Eliot's little known interest in the supernatural.

LADY AUDLEY'S SECRET
Mary E. Braddon

"Did she remember the day in which that fairy dower of beauty had first taught her to be selfish and cruel, indifferent to the joys and sorrows of others . . . ?"

Sir Michael Audley is captivated by his young and beautiful second wife. She has made a most advantageous match: once a governess, she is now mistress of Audley Court, a splendid and rambling mansion, and envy of the neighbourhood. Those who meet Lady Audley are fascinated by her, most particularly her husband's nephew, Robert. But his fascination begins to disturb him. For as he investigates the mysterious disappearance of his friend, George Talboys, he discovers that Lady Audley's beguiling charm masks the cold heart of a ruthless woman. This accomplished intrigue, first published in 1862, is Mary Braddon's most celebrated work. One of the greatest "sensation" novels ever written, *Lady Audley's Secret* shocked the Victorian public with its revelations of horrors at the very heart of respectable society and its most respectable women.

Mary E. Braddon (1835-1915) was born in London. She became a best-selling author with the publication of *Lady Audley's Secret* which went through eight editions in 1862 alone. Editor and publisher, author of over eighty works of fiction, with Wilkie Collins and Mrs Henry Wood she was a precursor of the modern thriller-writer and one of the most popular novelists of her day. Amongst her avid readers were Tennyson, Dickens, Thackeray and the young Henry James.